CRISS CROSS

CRISS CROSS

EVIE RHODES

Dafina Books

KENSINGTON PUBLISHING CORP.
http://www.kensingtonbooks.com

DAFINA BOOKS are published by

Kensington Publishing Corp.
850 Third Avenue
New York, NY 10022

All Kensington titles, imprints and distributed lines are available at special quantity discounts for bulk purchases for sales promotion, premiums, fund-raising, educational or institutional use.

Special book excerpts or customized printings can also be created to fit specific needs. For details, write or phone the office of the Kensington Special Sales Manager: Kensington Publishing Corp., 850 Third Avenue, New York, NY 10022. Attn. Special Sales Department. Phone: 1-800-221-2647.

Dafina Books and the Dafina logo Reg. U.S. Pat. & TM Off.

ISBN 0-7582-0872-3

First Kensington Trade Paperback Printing: February 2006
10 9 8 7 6 5 4 3 2 1

Printed in the United States of America

CRISS CROSS *is dedicated to The Lord Jesus Christ!*

Special Acknowledgments

To my husband, James Rhodes, you are the wind beneath my wings!

To my mother, Rozzie Lee Jackson, I've found my gift and learned how to use it. Rest in Peace.

To my daughter, Jamie Lynne Rhodes, thank you for all the times you read Criss Cross *and acted out the roles with me!*

To my son, James Rhodes, Jr., thank you for your consideration and sacrifice during the time I needed to write.

To my grandfather, Robert Lee Jackson, I love you Daddy. I always have!

To my mother-in-law, Susan Hackett, I consider you a treasure. Thank you for being a blessing. And for leading Jimmy and me to the water! Hallelujah!

To my dad, John Shannon, thank you for your support during the promotion of my book Expired. *I very much appreciate it. Much love!*

To a very special person, Linda Lepp, truly I could never say enough so let me keep it simple and just say, May the Lord Bless You!

A very special and heartwarming thanks to Karen Thomas, my editor, thank you for always preserving my voice. I love you for that!

A very special and heartwarming thanks to:
Robert G. (Bob) Diforio, my agent; Laurie Parkin, vice president; Nicole Bruce, editorial assistant; Jessica McLean-Ricketts, national sales rep; Kristine Mills-Noble, for another fine cover; Joan Schulhafer, director of publicity; Mary Pomponio, publicist; Lydia Stein, production editor; and last, but most certainly not least, Steven Zacharius, CEO of Kensington Publishing.

To all of you who are in the publishing chain from reading to editing to production to warehousing, to selling, to distribution it warms my heart to think of you. Thanks for sharing in making my dream a reality.

I thank you all for your contribution to my literary journey. Much love!

And to my readers, I wish you an extra special blessing. Many of you have written to me and you can never know what a blessing that is! Thank you from the bottom of my heart for supporting my stories. Godspeed!

To All Who Know Me I Remain, Standing in The Spirit!

CRISS CROSS

Chapter 1

1967
Newark, New Jersey

"Now and forever, Evelyn," Quentin's words were spoken hauntingly, softly into her ear. "Do you know what those two words mean?"

Hungrily and with total authority he pulled her closer to him.

"Umm." Evelyn moaned as she molded her body closer, tighter against his firm masculinity. She loved the absolute feel of him.

"They mean exactly what they say, now and forever. For you specifically they mean you will never escape."

Never escape? The words hung in the air menacingly. *Something was very wrong.*

The rain splashed over them. The wind blew her hair. It was the most sensual moment of her life, until the whispered words of a madman sounded in her ear. Their vibe and meaning slowly seeped through to her brain.

The night was soft, black and velvety. A torrential downpour soaked the streets of Newark, New Jersey, cleansing the gutters of the city's core. Ridding it of some of the trash but not all.

The street was deserted. Quentin and Evelyn stood in the park, in romantic isolation, a block away from Evelyn's house.

They had taken a walk after a great dinner. Suddenly the sky had let loose with a fury and so had Quentin. Evelyn was totally confused.

She had been enjoying his company. He had elegant manners as well as sophistication. She thought she might come to care deeply for him. She had spent some deeply moving time with him. Then he flipped on her. Like a light switch that someone had flicked off.

She stood on tiptoe in her bare feet. She had removed her sandals in the heat of the smoldering rainy sexuality that had her body awash. As she pressed her body against Quentin's, a subtle change took place without a hint of warning.

Quentin was crazy. He was threatening her. What did he mean she was never going to escape? Warning signals ignited in her head. A cold fear seized her body clashing with the hot, sexy heat rising from her womanhood.

Her thoughts rippled, like pebbles skipping across the water. Her brain was suddenly in total chaos. She tried to order her thoughts into something that made sense. It was no use. Her thoughts were running rampant.

One thing she did know. She couldn't have anything more to do with him. Something was wrong with him. He was like Dr. Jekyll and Mr. Hyde.

Evelyn pulled back. She stared at Quentin Curry as though he'd lost his mind. "Let go of me." A clammy foreboding crawled up and down her skin. She shivered. Goose bumps began to sprout on her arms.

Quentin gripped her tighter. The force of his fingers left imprints in her skin. "Can't do that, Evelyn. Didn't you hear me? I said now and forever." He laughed at the bewilderment and utter lack of comprehension that flashed across her face.

A sense of unreality dug its clutches into Evelyn. Quentin's once expressive eyes were now only twin holes of black nothingness. Gone were any traces of the warmth and compassion that had embraced her earlier.

"You're crazy," she stuttered. " I want you out of my life. Let go of me."

Quentin shook his head. "What you want and what you get are two different things, Evelyn. You're never going to leave me. And I'm never going to leave you. Don't you get it? I said there will never be an escape for you. I always say what I mean. And, I always, *always*, mean what I say."

"No. You're a maniac. Let go of me!" she screamed. Her words blew away on the fury of the winds of the rain, as though a great sea was carrying them away.

Looking into his face, a wave of senselessness rushed over her. She spat a rush of words in his face. "I changed my mind about being with you. You're not who I thought you were."

"You changed your mind?"

Quentin looked up at the stormy skies. "Did you say you changed your mind? You don't change your mind Evelyn, unless I change it for you understood?" Quentin words were cold and precise. His voice never raised by a note.

Now, Evelyn knew two things: real fear and the fact that she needed to get away from him.

A surge of strength rose up in her. It was a strength born out of desperation. She wrenched her body free from Quentin's hold and ran wildly down the street. Her legs and feet were bare. Her sandals were long forgotten. Long wet strands of hair clung to her head and face.

The echo of her bare feet striking the wet pavement provided her with the rhythmic chaos that spurred her on. Evelyn blew the hair out of her eyes. She willed her legs to pump harder, faster as a numbness clawed at her body.

No way could she stop.

She looked briefly behind her. She panted as she picked up her pace, sprinting toward safety, which loomed not far in the distance.

Quentin Curry was a powerful, arrogant, and magnetic man. He was at the height of his physicality. His limbs were long and lithe. His carriage was tall and erect. He possessed a demeanor that indicated fierce pride.

He watched Evelyn run down the street. He was not at all concerned about her temporary escape. In fact, he wasn't the least bit perturbed.

Quentin was a man of many layers with a sadistic streak a mile long. His extreme confidence bordered on a God-like level. He was a man who knew his own power and one who had come into power by refusing to obey any boundaries but his own. Accustomed to getting his own way, he knew he had time.

Lazily, a sardonic smile crept across his face. His was a face that could have been sculpted by one of the masters. His face was masterful in the pure architecture of it, in the chiseled lines that outlined his features. It was a face with many textures and layers that he used at will.

Quentin wondered why people didn't realize they couldn't run from their fate.

He studied the picture that was Evelyn. He knew he had chosen carefully, oh, ever so carefully. Evelyn was the only child of deceased parents who left her with enough money that she would never have to worry about it in her lifetime.

She was a loner. Very isolated for one so young, always preferring her own company to that of others. She spent most of her time rummaging in bookstores and in the dusty corners of various libraries. The single link that connected her to the world was her writing.

Ah yes, her writing; perhaps a most useful tool.

She didn't have any real friends. All of her friends, imaginary to be sure, and relationships resided between the pages of books. Her friends were in the notes of the music she loved so much. That was the extent of it.

Evelyn stumbled in the wet street. She threw her hands out in front of her body to regain her balance. Her legs ached, throbbed actually with pain.

Or was it with fear?

She didn't know. "Legs, please don't fail me now," she whispered desperately. She had never been so scared in her life.

A stray cat ran out from its shelter into the rain. He caused Evelyn to practically jump out of her skin. She turned to look behind her, finding no sign of Quentin. She took a deep breath to quell her quivering body and kept running. She looked around the deserted street. There was no sign of life on the street, just her. "Somebody help," she whispered. "Somebody. Please help." There was no one to hear her.

*　　*　　*

Quentin lounged in the park contemplating his plan. He knew Evelyn thought he was behind her, chasing her. That was enough to keep her where he wanted her. He was a chaser, though not in the way she would expect. He could chase her without moving a muscle, just as effectively, more in fact, as if he had run after her.

Anyway he knew there would be no prying into the changes she was about to undergo. He thought about the Reverend Erwin Jackson, but quickly dismissed the thought as being of little consequence.

Reverend Erwin Jackson was Evelyn's minister. His was the one relationship she seemed to foster. The reverend's presence might lend a bit of an edge to the game.

Breeding was important and Evelyn's lineage showed good breeding. He'd done his checklist centuries in advance. He'd been waiting for her, for her arrival, for her birth. Now it was time. He'd been watching. Watching was what he did. Watching and observing were part of his highly honed and sharpened skills.

He knew her womb was young and untouched. She was pure. This was very necessary to his plan. He could not funnel through tainted goods.

He smiled. He was satisfied with the wisdom of his choice. One had to create his own opportunities. And he had certainly created his. In his supreme arrogance, he settled on a single thought: The girl is in for the treat of her life and she's running from me. Quentin shook his head in amazement.

He dropped his cigarette lighter. He reached to pick it up. Tattooed in the back of his right hand was an "X." He lit a cigarette as the mist of the rainy night shrouded him.

The predator in him inched its way to the forefront. The pull of it tingled through his body. The sleek black panther of spirit he possessed was now on the prowl. It was lurking just beneath the surface.

Evelyn heaved air in great gulps as she raced up the steps of the Victorian house she had inherited from her parents. It was one of the last of its kind left in the Newark neighborhood.

The house carried a certain presence. It had an ominous, yet old elegant air about it. It was wrapped in an air of quiet dignity. In the dark of this night, it was possessed with a spirit of stillness.

Evelyn fumbled with her keys looking wildly behind her. She tried to jam the key in the lock. She fumbled again. The wet keys slipped from her shaking fingers and dropped to the porch floor. She picked them up. She worked at steadying herself. She tried again. The lock clicked. She bolted through the front door. She slammed it shut and locked it behind her.

Evelyn raced into the solarium. She locked that door too. She stood trembling as little pools of water formed on the floor from her bare wet feet.

She was completely unaware of the youth, sensual beauty and vitality that radiated from her. Evelyn was a petite young woman with several feet of dark, thick black locks of hair. She had beautiful translucent brown eyes. And, flawless coffee-colored skin with dimpled cheeks. She ran her hands up and down her arms, grappling with a terror the likes of which she had never known.

Quentin lay splayed on the skylight of the solarium. His gaze was hypnotic as it devoured the sensual Evelyn Jordan-Wells. He reveled in her image, enjoying the feel of the hunt.

His loins ached with the thought of having her, possessing her. A groan of pleasure escaped his lips. Evelyn's fear was a tangible thing to him. He breathed it in.

Quentin's eyes were liquid pools of midnight black as he stared through the glass at Evelyn.

Evelyn, sensing his presence, looked up. Her gaze riveted on Quentin. She shook like a leaf on a tree.

Abruptly, torrential rain, wind and shattering glass engulfed her as Quentin crashed through into the solarium.

Evelyn hyperventilated in her fear. But Quentin's hypnotic stare changed the very rhythm of her breathing. Slowly her labored breathing broke into an even pattern.

Seductively sweet and with a hint of red-hot passion, Quentin touched Evelyn, ever so lightly. "Evelyn Jordan-Wells," he said. Her name rolled off his tongue like sweet licorice candy.

"Hide and seek. You think you can hide from me? Umm, a game. I like games, Evelyn. I created them you know." Evelyn shrank back from him. Quentin allowed it for the time being.

He continued speaking as though there had been no physical

interruption. "I especially like games that change the course of history. Games that upset the balance of power. Sensual, sexual and exquisite games, Evelyn. You and I will play. You do want to play with me. Don't you?" His voice had a languid purr to it. It held the promise of a lullaby.

He grabbed her, pulling her to him. He put his lips close to her ear. A deep rage settled over him. He turned his head. It twisted around like rubber. His eyes produced a laser glow that destroyed everything in its path.

"Come on, dance with me, Evelyn," Quentin purred.

The beautiful greenery and antiques that endowed the solarium room ripped right out of the floor at the force of Quentin's gaze.

His gaze swept around the room. The walls exploded. The windows blew out. Evelyn broke loose. She backed away from Quentin. A scream erupted from her throat as if a volcano had burst forth.

She crouched and cowered in the face of an evil that was so tangible she could reach out and touch it. Nothing in her sheltered life had prepared her for the darkness that had breached her world. In its face, she was completely helpless.

Evelyn briefly looked up. She stared at Quentin as though she had never seen him before. In truth she hadn't. Shock contorted every limb in her body.

The monster in Quentin had unleashed before her eyes. It had replaced the man that she thought she might love. Standing in front of her was a total stranger. It was a stranger who was in possession of a dark and lethal power. He was not of this world. Evelyn recoiled in shock.

Searing, white-hot, glittering flashes of light exploded in her brain. She searched the crevices of her mind desperately for a place to hide. There was no refuge. There was nothing for her to cling to.

A chord of deep fear struck within her. She babbled out loud, "Jesus Lord, Jesus Lord, Jesus Lord."

The sound of her babbling added fuel to Quentin's fire. He burned a flaming "X" into the wall. "I AM THE LORD! I am your Lord, Evelyn!" Softly switching gears he said, "Though my name is not Jesus."

His eyes burned a hole through her shirt. It sizzled but didn't burn her skin.

Returning to his former state he said, "Don't you ever forget that

I AM THE LORD! I am Lord over both life and death. I will not be forgotten. Do you hear me? No one will ever forget me. Everyone will know I was here." Quentin fixed his twin holes of blackness on Evelyn.

Evelyn sobbed. She gulped air. Raw fear held her in its grip. Astonishment was her new companion. She could feel Quentin crawling around in her mind, poking, feeling. He found it all. Every secret. Her mind lay spread-eagle naked before him.

His presence was a live wire as he insinuated himself into her thoughts. "My Lord." The words rushed from her lips as if they belonged to someone else. She was barely aware of speaking them.

Quentin laughed. "You're coming along, Evelyn. You're coming along nicely. It pleases me when people use my title."

Evelyn went mute. She was struck dumb by the supreme arrogance emanating from this creature.

"I am a Prince, Evelyn. The Prince. You've heard of me. You've read about me. Yet you don't believe in me. Few people do. It's what makes me powerful. You're a perfect specimen of the stupidest species to inhabit earth. I know animals smarter than you."

Quentin threw his head back and roared, "I am what I am! Can't you see me?! You don't believe your own eyes?! Well, here I am! In the flesh! I am my own MAKER!"

He paused. "I am also YOURS!"

He pointed to the masterpiece he had seared into the wall. The flaming "X" glowed with a light of its own.

"This is my legacy, Evelyn. It is my mark. It will travel through the generations of my seed to come. It is a life force. It is what makes me eternal. Didn't they teach you all about that in Sunday school?"

He stooped down so he could be at eye level with Evelyn. "Take a look around, because you will spend a great deal of time on these very premises, Evelyn. You will never leave this house again. Oh, no. You will not ever leave. Because if you do . . ." He reached for a handful of her wet hair. He forced her face up to his.

His gaze bore into her. "If you ever try to leave you will die! You will die a death more vicious than the wildest imagination can conjure up. Painfully and slowly, I will release life from your body. Until you beg for death. Until you seek its face. I will kill you and anything you love. Understood? Look at the mark."

His voice now held the musical tempo of soothing waters. "Look at it I said."

Evelyn struggled to rip her gaze from him. She looked at the flaming, spirited "X" seared into the wall. The mark swam like a watery illusion before her eyes.

"You've been chosen to be the carrier of my legend. In your womb the seed of the "X" will be implanted for generations to come. You, Evelyn, will raise a warrior. Remember the number six. Don't forget it because it's a very important part of your future." His words echoed through the chambers of her being.

Venom rose from the depths of her belly. Hatred swelled inside her. Refusal bubbled from the depths of her soul at the despicable evil. It spewed forth from her lips. She warred with him in a single word. "No!" She pushed him so hard he stumbled backwards.

The tail of a reptile leaped from his eyes. It lashed around her neck choking her. It left a trailing red welt on her skin. As quickly as it emerged, it withdrew. Evelyn gagged. She wet herself.

Quentin was unperturbed. He got up and in her face just a little bit closer. Calmly he told her, "Yes."

He turned his attention to the "X." It burned brighter under the heat of his satanic gaze. Light streamed from his eyes.

He looked at her. Hot sensuality replaced the light streaming from his eyes, an animal scent of musk rose from the heat of his body.

Quentin slowly licked the outer parameters of Evelyn's lips. He was all lithe sensuality as he gently stroked her wet hair. He kissed the tears from her cheeks.

Evelyn rebuffed his very touch. Her skin crawled from the touch of the beast. Her insides heaved. Then something inside her cracked. It broke down. It disconnected. She lost the last of the tentative hold. She couldn't handle it.

Once again she reached out seeking solace in a corner of her mind she never knew was there. This time the corner embraced her with warm and welcoming arms. It was a place of peace, quietness and refuge.

She floated away as the beast mauled and devoured her body.

Chapter 2

Some weeks later, Evelyn sat in the warmth of her parlor staring across at Reverend Erwin Jackson. It was a lavishly appointed room, spacious and encompassed by high ceilings.

The wallpaper was decorated with astonishing hand-stenciled details of vines and birds.

The fireplace created warmth in the room as the flames crackled, although heavy brocade drapes were pulled against the windows, keeping out the day's sunlight.

The room was scattered with sofas, chairs, footstools and tables. Collections of recordings of music by Frederic Francois Chopin, Ludwig Van Beethoven, and Franz Liszt sat with a book of poems by Emily Jane Bronte.

Evelyn inherited the wonderful collection from her parents. On a normal day she would sit in this room, listening to Chopin, Beethoven, or Liszt while writing longhand on her yellow legal pad.

However, this was not a normal day. Her collections were silent. The silence was loud, almost unbearable. She thought of the collections as her friends. They had been there in her times of need. It seemed as if somewhere along the way in their instrumentation, they had drawn for her a musical pattern that would shape her life, with their peaks and valleys.

Today there were no symphonic poems and melodies being released. Today there were no crashing crescendos playing to match the rhythm of her pen.

The composers had composed their last notes, she supposed, laying the final groundwork for this stage. Now it was her cue. "Reverend Jackson, thank you for coming on such short notice . . ." Her voice trailed off on an uneven note as though she had suddenly lost her thought.

The reverend observed her closely. "You are free to call me, anytime, day or night. You are aware of that."

"Yes. I know. Thank you," Evelyn sighed. She lapsed into her own thoughts. The room had always provided her with a special feeling of belonging and passion.

The parlor had, in the past, inspired her to great heights. The very feel of the room, its atmosphere, helped her to discover an existence and connect to her writing at a level and depth she hadn't known was possible. Now it seemed as if it had withdrawn its comforts from her.

Of every room in the house this room was her very favorite. At times she could hear the laughter and joy of the past that was now sealed, solid and frozen, in memory only, within the walls. Within those walls was life, the foundation of her life from a different time.

She shivered in the shawl draped around her shoulders. The room no longer held that special warmth for her. It was as though a vacuum had sucked it all out. She tried to bring her vision in focus.

Fragments of words swirled as though she were on an international call listening to the faraway echo of a voice on the other end, which had suddenly been disconnected.

Groping for something to say, she leveled a stare at the reverend. "How are things at the orphanage?"

"Fine. In fact we have a new little boy who has taken quite a liking to me. He's been helping to clean the chapel. The child sits at my feet while I'm preparing scriptures. I've been reading to him." The reverend shook his head. "Amazing little fellow he is. Who knows? Maybe he'll grow up to be a missionary. He comes from a tough background but he's eager to hear about the Lord, so you never know what will happen."

"No. I guess you never do," Evelyn replied.

The muted lighting in the room cast a faint glow and Evelyn found her attention wandering to watch the kaleidoscope of colors dancing from the stained glass figurine sitting on the table between her and Reverend Jackson. She reclined in her seat, crossing her legs at the ankles.

The reverend studied Evelyn. He wondered at the turmoil and conflict that were trading places across her frozen features. He had been her minister since she was a child. Never before had he sensed such despair in her. Nevertheless he was a trusted confidant, a servant of God. So, he sipped from his cup of coffee and waited patiently.

"Reverend Jackson, there are some changes taking place and I, umm, well, I wanted to talk to you about them."

"Of course. What sort of changes are you speaking about?"

Evelyn's attention strayed. She didn't answer right away. Finally, she struggled to pull her gaze from the dancing colors of the glass figurine. She took a sip from her cup.

She looked at the reverend. Her throat constricted and went mute. Her vocal chords froze and not a word came out. She cleared her throat. The reverend didn't rush her.

She knew there was no way to cushion what was on her mind. Her need went beyond the very grain of all she believed. She needed the endorsement of Reverend Jackson although, in her wildest fantasies, she didn't imagine she would receive it.

However, she was determined to press forward. She drew her shoulders straighter. Then they slumped and she faltered. Indecision rose up in her. How could she go on? How could she tell the reverend? She must. Pinpricks of rage stabbed at her brain. She was obsessed by the knowledge of the monster that was growing in her womb. Her hands trembled.

This thought spurred her on. The very idea of ridding herself of the monster had temporarily stayed her fear. She imagined what it would feel like if she could beat Quentin, even at the risk of losing her own life.

In this one act, she could take away from him the very thing that he wanted. She looked at the reverend. At last she said, "I'm pregnant. I can't have this baby. I need an abortion." The words tumbled out of her mouth after being pent up for so long.

When she uttered the words, a high-pitched screech sailed through the air that only she could hear. A low growl emitted from the fireplace.

Reverend Jackson blinked. He reined in his astonishment. Evelyn had always been so upright. It was all he could do to imagine her in an unwed relationship.

He considered the early loss of her parents, the accidental death of her maiden aunt, her last living relative. He supposed it was not surprising that she had sought companionship. Her announcement of pregnancy was vividly shocking.

Nevertheless, he assumed a calm air of solidarity. This was a steadiness that had served him for many years. Any trace of the surprise he felt was expunged from his voice before he spoke. "Evelyn, you know I can't advise the termination of a pregnancy," he said.

Evelyn shifted to the end of her cushioned chair. She fought hard to ignore the screeching, the growling. "You don't understand Reverend. The relationship, it isn't . . . it just isn't . . . I just don't want it. I have to get rid of this baby."

The glass figurine beckoned to get Evelyn's attention. There were no longer muted colors of beauty streaming from it. The figurine had been turned upside down on its head. The tail of a reptile was choking its neck. The only color streaming from it was red. Red blood.

Evelyn bit her lip to keep from screaming. She bit it so hard she broke the skin and could feel the blood seeping into her mouth.

The reverend was taken aback by the venom-tinged words: "I have to get rid of this baby." Evelyn sounded like a stranger.

He didn't condone this pregnancy. But considering the girl was alone he would have expected a different reaction. Her vehement rejection of the child growing in her womb was quite disturbing.

He placed a soothing hand over Evelyn's. Her hands were ice cold and rock hard. They were trembling with the force of an earthquake.

He said, "I can't give this my blessing. I can't advise the termination of a pregnancy. It just can't be done under any circumstances. God has a way of working things out, my child. Let Him do it. In His time and in His way."

Risking a glance at the figurine Evelyn found it had righted itself. Once again it was glowing with a rainbow beauty of colors. There was no tail of a reptile choking its neck. The neck of the figurine was flawless in its slender elegance. The screeching and growling had stopped.

Evelyn pulled her hand away. She was unable to control the trembling that robbed her of her agility. She wanted to pick up her coffee cup but found that her thought processes had disconnected from her limbs. She lacked the ability to complete such an innocent task.

Willing her mental processes back into control over the physical, she smoothed her skirt and felt relieved at the simple movement.

She wished she could believe the reverend's words. She wished she could remember all she had been taught. But lately it seemed as though whatever knowledge she once possessed had deserted her. It was as if thieves had broken in and stolen it.

Reverend Jackson's God, who used to be her God as well, suddenly held no comfort for her. She desperately wanted to believe. She couldn't. She had found she was sorely lacking the ability to see anything except the darkness that had shrouded and invaded her life.

"Reverend Jackson, there must be some exception." She stumbled over the words, almost gagging on them.

The reverend gave her his most comforting look. When he spoke his words were tinged with a hint of authority. "I'm sorry. There aren't any exceptions, Evelyn."

Evelyn sighed. She was deeply disappointed, abandoned and scared. She didn't argue or dispute the reverend. She had expected exactly this.

A sense of pure desolation washed over her at the reverend's words. She knew somewhere in her religion there was a cornerstone, a rock, but she didn't know how to get to it. Those thoughts seemed to belong to someone she used to know, like a best friend she had lost contact with.

Her face crumbled for a fraction of a second. The reverend watched her war with herself to win back her composure. He sighed deeply.

Finally, drawing on sheer willpower, Evelyn arranged her posture to reflect a strength she didn't feel. "If I am left with no choice, then there is something I need to share with you. Something that must not ever be revealed outside of this room."

Evelyn could taste the bitterness, rising like bile in her throat. She was about to subject herself to a scrutiny she wasn't sure she could handle.

Quentin was the outward visible sign of her worst fear, manifested in the flesh. He was the ultimate culmination of every fear she had ever known. He was a full-blown breathing nightmare.

Reverend Jackson was one of the most solid people she knew. Yet, even he would be hard-pressed to believe her story. It didn't matter. There was no way she could carry the weight of this alone. So she decided to cast her line out onto spiritual waters.

Evelyn looked around the room. She lowered her voice to a whisper. She said, "Never, Reverend, never can my words leave this room."

An involuntary tremor passed through the reverend as her words were spoken. As though the very finger of God were touching his soul. He was drawn as if by a magnet to stare at the blazing flames in the fireplace.

He blinked. He had never experienced such an eternal feeling. The reverend searched his mind for scriptural support, which was always the support he sought. Finding none, he stared at Evelyn while taking a deep breath.

Looking beyond her, he suddenly knew he was unprepared for the magnitude of the burden she was about to lay at his doorstep. Just as he'd always known instinctively that one day his ministry would become pivotal to some event not of his making.

He allowed himself the briefest moment of solace by closing his eyes. When he opened them he looked directly at Evelyn and said, "Speak, child."

Chapter 3

1999

Thirty-two-years later, the seed implanted in Evelyn's womb had become a man. He was the product of her worst fears. He was the epitome of her highest joy. Like a pendulum, Evelyn's fate had swung high and low.

He was sprung from a foundation of pain. He was derived through great deception. He was born in the shadows of darkness, in murky waters. He was Evelyn's son. He was her pride and joy. His name was Micah Jordan-Wells. And he had yet to know his title.

Evelyn had never told him about the circumstances surrounding his conception. She had not spoken to him of his father. She had shielded him from an awful truth.

She thought what he didn't know couldn't hurt him. Their lives were crafted in the simple act of denial.

She had made a singular choice. She took the uncomplicated path. Then fate intervened and dared to display its uncontrollable factors.

Micah Jordan-Wells was battling his own demons. The sins of the past were visited upon him. The truth of his existence hovered nearby. The truth waited. It waited patiently. Then it struck. It cast its net in the deep of the night upon Micah Jordan-Wells.

It was dark. Pitch-black dark. Hot mist rose from the ground around Micah's feet. He struggled to free his hands and feet from the roped wired bounds. The muscles in his biceps tensed. They coiled. Micah was wired tight to a chair. He slithered around like a cobra in a desperate attempt to be free.

It was intensely hot in the room. The temperature soared beyond anything normal. Sweat dripped, poured into his eyes, skewing his vision. He tasted the salt of it in his mouth.

His jerking around caused the wires to slice through his flesh. Red spots of blood oozed from his wrists and ankles. Then there was a sound like the roar of a rushing wind. An ear-shattering explosion burst forth. His ears popped.

Micah sat very still. He listened. He tried to identify the direction of the sound.

Red-orange light burst forth through the darkness. A flaming ball of fire rushed him. With the speed of light, it was on him. He howled. A mix of denial, defiance and terror discharged from his throat.

Someone laughed. Mocked him. He heard a deep baritone voice. It held no life. It held no feeling. It echoed up to him from a deep pit. "Micah! Micah!" It drew him in, sucking him down into its tunnel a mere instant before he would have been engulfed in flames.

A flaming "X" shone through the darkness. Molten heat seared it into the cement floor. The "X" slowly ascended. Then it branded itself over Micah's body merging with him. Gut-wrenching sounds of pure agony gushed from Micah's mouth. Buckets of vomit poured forth through his parched lips.

He scooted his chair backward to resist the merging. He twisted. He turned, trying to gain some distance from the frightening mark. It was all over him. He shuddered. Stark fear drenched his body. The smell of his own musk reached his nostrils.

Micah's dehydrated body jerked spastically. He sat up in bed. Sweat-dripping terror of the darkest kind drenched his body. His mind whirled in confusion.

He looked around. The room slowly came into focus. He had emerged. He freed his wet body from the twisted sheets.

He jumped out of bed and strode to the shower. He knew it was time to face the real demons of his world. There were enough of them; he didn't need to conjure up more in his sleep.

Micah Jordan-Wells was a high profile, very celebrated homicide detective in Newark, New Jersey. He was a man who had done battle with a great many of Newark's dragons. He'd affectionately been given the nickname of the Dragon Slayer by Newark's elite corps of the press. Right now he was the darling of the media for reeling in a man called Silky who had wreaked terror in the streets of Newark.

Silky had created horror in their hearts. He had numbed the minds of Newark's citizens and police force. In short he had scandalized them into electric outrage.

Silky didn't just commit crimes; he gave the impression of creating them like an artist creates a portrait—murder by design. His murders were like hideous paintings, created by a master who wants you to marvel at the boldness of his strokes and guess at the illusions he has hinted at.

Silky possessed a darkness of spirit that leapt out from the carcass of his victims and screamed for justice. The callousness with which he performed made him unparalleled in the annals of crime.

Micah was still grappling with the tail end of Silky's case, which was taking its place in Newark's crime history as something akin to notorious.

He turned the spray nozzle in the shower to full force. He shivered as the shock of ice-cold needles sprayed his body into rigid alertness. As the water rained over his body the "X" beckoned, once again. It summoned him. There was no resistance in him because there could be none.

It was happening again. A visionary connection between him and an horrific act manifested in his flesh, swamping his being, connecting him to a dark and evil path. The inhabitation of the person's eyes he looked through made him shudder. The things he saw made him weep. They were his eyes and yet they were not. Physically the eyes belonged to someone else, spiritually he carried the burden of seeing and feeling what they were doing. They were his hands and yet they were not. Who was he fooling? He was there. The burden of the act was his.

The immeasurable joy of the act of murder swept through his limbs and merged with his being. It was another woman, another victim, and yet another masterpiece.

She was a prized photograph. Her high-heeled feet kicked wildly. Her legs were bare beneath the gold dress. Moonlight streaked across the shadows of darkness in the room. Tied around her throat was a pair of silk panty hose. He pulled tighter and tighter. The "X" seared itself into her forehead.

Her wild kicking slowed. Her legs flopped beneath her. The last shred of life drained from her body. One of her gold silk-strapped, high-heeled shoes fell off her foot. Her body went limp. It was final.

He stroked the soft silk of the panty hose. He loved the feel of the silky softness between his fingers. Stark fear sprayed from her eyes. Only now it was frozen in its portrayal.

He smiled. The rapture was upon him.

The mark of the "X" pulsated within his body. His skin gleamed with the shine of it. He took one look around. His final gaze rested on the framed picture of a six-year-old boy.

Chapter 4

There was a sizzling current of anticipation in the air outside of Newark's courtroom, as well as a deep rippling wave of destiny riding on a strident undercurrent.

The penalty phase of the trial for Silky—also known as David Edward Stokes—was just beginning. It had brought out the masses in full force.

Present were the common citizens of Newark who sought peace of mind and justice, as well as law enforcement officers from bordering cities who had kept abreast of the chase as Micah tracked the elusive Silky.

The media had marshaled itself in full force. Everyone was waiting for the final hammer to sound on Silky's murdering spree.

Impeccably tailored in a dark pin-striped suit, a wine-colored silk tie, sporting soft Italian leather wing-tipped shoes that matched his tie, and a low hair cut that showed off the natural soft wave of his hair, Micah Jordan-Wells cut a dashing picture of self-assuredness and confidence.

Micah was a dangerously handsome man. His face had been cast with classic features. His coffee-colored skin was velvety looking in its smooth texture and his eyebrows had a natural wavy arch to them.

He had long dark sweeping lashes that fringed a pair of eyes that were penetrating as well as observant. Yet, there was a light of kindness that shown through from time to time, capturing you in the depth and brilliance of their light brown coloring.

Charisma clung to Micah as though he had been given a permanent patent on it.

He stood just outside the courtroom door in the hallway with his partner, Nugent Lewis, otherwise known as Nuggie to those near and dear.

Nugent was about as laid-back as they come. He was made of solid stuff. Never easy to ruffle, Nugent observed the world through a self-created distance. He was also Micah's right-hand man. They were closer than brothers.

As two of Silky's counsels approached the courtroom they both gave an inward sigh upon spotting Micah Jordan-Wells, who was clearly king of the day, standing in front of the courtroom.

Micah slid smoothly into script as they stopped in front of him. He pinned his sights first on Judd Nelson who was the lead counsel. "You should never have taken this case, Judd, and you know it."

The second attorney, Rick Bowker, jumped in before Judd could reply. "Ever the expert. Right, Micah?"

Nugent laughed. "I would never have figured you clean-cut prominent guys for ambulance chasers, but . . ." Nugent shrugged his shoulders and let his sentence trail off leaving a clear rebuff in the air.

Judd Nelson said, "You want to reel in your ego just a bit, Micah?" He ignored Nugent.

Judd's entire law firm, including the partners, had thought the high-profile case of Silky would be easily locked down. They had looked forward to bucking horns with the charismatic Micah Jordan-Wells.

They had counted on it to pitch their law firm as well as the presiding attorneys into the national spotlight, which it had. What they hadn't counted on was being made to look like national fools.

It was a simple case of murder by insanity, or so they'd thought. But it hadn't turned out like that. They had assembled their experts. Patrick Hayes, the prosecutor, had discredited each of them during the trial.

The end result was that now Micah stood looking at them knowing they would have given their right arms to be any place else and in his conceit he was being less than gracious about it. The press hovered nearby, catching the whiff of a possible catfight.

Derrick Holt, the *Star-Ledger* newspaper's crime reporter smelled a golden opportunity arising. Never one to let it pass, he strolled over and took the tension to the next level by complimenting Micah.

"Micah, dazzling footwork man, just dazzling. It's been brought to my attention that your police work and testimony are being written about in countless publications around the country, and it's slated to become a documented case study on the university circuit."

Derrick stuck out his hand and Micah reached for it.

Micah smiled. Meekly he said, "It looks like you have more information than me, Mr. Holt, but I certainly hope the capture of such a dangerous criminal as David Stokes will assist in precedent for other killers that prey on innocent society."

It was all Judd Nelson could do to keep his breakfast down and not roll his eyes heavenward in front of the media who had slunk closer and were beginning to record the conversation as well as snap pictures.

Judd's job had been to paint Silky as insane, to say that a man who committed such heinous crimes couldn't be sane. They had done it in countless other cases. This one was different. The jury didn't buy it.

Immediately upon Micah's response an NBC news reporter jumped in. She stuck a microphone in Micah's face and said, "Micah, your performance at the trial was one that courtroom legends are made of."

Before Micah could respond, the CBS correspondent said, "You turned the witness chair into something akin to sainthood. How does it feel?"

Derrick Holt, not intending to lose the momentum he had created said, "Yeah Micah, you and the DA were in perfect harmony. If this wasn't a courtroom trial I might have thought I was at a symphony the way you and Patrick Hayes, orchestrated the details of this case."

Everyone laughed his or her agreement with the exception of Judd Nelson and Rick Bowker. They stood trying to maintain their composure and hang on to the remaining shreds of their dignity as the press ignored them.

And there was no way they could excuse themselves from the crowd gracefully. They were caught up in a riptide and Micah Jordan-Wells was reigning supreme.

The NBC correspondent said to Micah, "The trial was like virtual reality. You put the jurors in the victim's skin. They were living the murders by simulation. That's quite a feat. I have to say that in the many trials I have covered I haven't ever witnessed the singular bond you seemed to have with the jury. The city of Newark and its residents are grateful to you."

"There really isn't a need for that," Micah said. "That's my job. It's what I do."

John Morrison, head of Newark's homicide division and known to friend and foe alike simply as Wolfgang, walked up in the midst of the media circus.

He smiled. "It's time to go into the courtroom."

The court's deputy sheriff nodded his appreciation. He had been just about to approach the mob to shepherd them in.

Micah turned immediately on his heels. He strode into the courtroom with Nugent right behind him and Wolfgang, who was Micah's superior, stuck close to his side.

The media turned off their electronic communications, as they were not allowed to use them in the courtroom. No cameras, no cell phones, no pagers, and no beepers unless you wanted to be strictly barred from the proceedings as well as reprimanded.

The media did not even have a chance to question Wolfgang; the penalty phase of the trial was ready to begin.

They all filed into the courtroom to hear the final sentencing of David Edward Stokes and to celebrate the end of his horrific, serial murdering marathon.

Chapter 5

The stage had been set as they all filed into the courtroom. The defendant known as Silky, Newark's mystifying, calculating, serial killer, was already chained and seated at the defense table.

He sat with the relaxed posture of someone who was free, as if the chains that bound him were of no consequence and could only hold him if he allowed them to do so.

Silky's jet-black, kinky, thick hair was pulled back in a ponytail. Knots of long, black, unkempt hair trailed down his back. His eyes were mesmerizing and fixed as they took in the atmosphere.

He had cast a pall of malefic doom over Newark by branding his victims as if they were cattle. He left his signature firmly engraved in the skin of his victims like an illuminating light. He had created a frightful trail that was like a beacon shining straight into hell.

There was the heady feel of the hunt in the air, as the penalty phase of the trial began. Silky turned to look at Micah and winked. Micah gave him a ready-to-rip-your-head-off look.

Judge Leiberman was at the entryway to the courtroom. He was a stern-looking, no-nonsense man. He looked at Silky. The man was a monster. How could he be a creation of nature? In his entire career, the judge had never witnessed so black a soul so up-close.

The bailiff shouted, "All rise, please." The people in the courtroom rose to their feet as Judge Leiberman approached and stood behind the old mahogany bench where he had presided over many a trial.

The judge banged his gavel. "You may be seated now. Will the defendant, David Edward Stokes, please stand."

Silky slowly climbed to his shackled feet. He rose regally and majestically, chains and all. His attorneys, Judd Nelson and Rick Bowker, flanked him.

Judge Leiberman looked at him with disgust. Silky was unaffected by this. "Would you like to address the court before your sentencing, Mr. Stokes?"

Silky turned slowly. He swept the crowd with his intense gaze. He turned back to face the judge. "Yeah. Kiss my ass."

Judge Leiberman shook his head. "You have absolutely no remorse or regrets. Do you, young man?"

Silky's eyes fluttered shut as he relived the sensuality. The sheer adrenaline pumping power of the moment he strangled and marked a woman. He loved the feel of the portraits he could conjure up at will. It was a self-induced motion picture.

His victims danced before his shut lids in all their terrorized glory. The lips of the women were bloated from strangulation. The silk panty hose knotted around their throats sent a stroke of pride trembling through his flesh.

An "X" was branded on their foreheads. In fascinating succession, they leapt before his eyes, each and every one of his six masterpieces.

Silky tugged himself reluctantly from the warmth of his reveries. He lowered his voice to a sultry, seductive tone. "I regret that I don't have enough time to tie my panty hose around the necks of the whores in this courtroom today." There was a single gasp from the audience.

"That's enough," Judge Leiberman said.

"I'll tell you when it's enough," Silky replied.

Judge Leiberman puffed up with indignant anger. "How dare you? This is my courtroom—"

"—This is your hell. All of the judgments that you've made . . . my dear judge will come back to you. That's the beauty of being me. By that which you judge, so shall you be judged."

Silky leaped aerobically, chains and all, in the air. His body twirled in a full complete circle. He landed on the defense table on his feet. "You will burn!"

"Get him down!" Judge Leiberman shouted.

"I am wrath! And you shall see it!"

Silky's attorneys were in a state of shock. They jumped away from the counsel table. The crowd gasped. People were shouting. The police guards wrestled Silky down from the table to the floor. They fell in a sprawling heap. Finally, they pulled on his chains, yanking him to his feet, back into a position of respect.

"I'll be back!" Silky shouted. "Only this time I'll be eating your young! Like I said! I regret I don't have enough time to tie my panty hose around the necks of the whores in this courtroom today!"

Silky laughed—the sound was like nails scraping against a blackboard. The high-pitched wail soared through the courtroom. The octaves of his voice climbed higher and higher. The sound of it was so dark it produced a scattering of shivers throughout the audience.

Outrage and pandemonium broke out in the courtroom. Judge Leiberman banged his gavel in fury, restoring quiet and order to his court.

The judge pronounced his sentence. "You have been found guilty on all counts of first-degree premeditated murder. You will be put to death." Judge Leiberman banged his gavel a final time. "Court is adjourned."

Silky's laugh was the only lingering sound in the room. The media ran to file their reports. The spectators breathed an uneasy sigh of relief. It wasn't easy to get the sticky feel of Silky off their skin.

Silky finally stopped laughing. He tilted his head proudly and knowingly.

Patrick Hayes closed his file. Micah Jordan-Wells glided smoothly from his seat with Wolfgang and Nugent in tow. He strolled arrogantly down the aisle.

Two police guards dragged Silky away from the counsel table. The chains that bound him clinked and clanged. The sentencing had been passed.

Silky seized the moment and shouted, "Micah!" His voice quaked with a deep and guttural resonance. The sound of Silky's voice killed the chaos in the room.

The media went into a feeding frenzy at the mere sound of Silky's voice. They committed a serious breach of conduct, but they could not and would not miss this story. Besides, court was adjourned. They smelled blood in Silky's voice and they were ready.

Flashbulbs popped off in Micah's as well as Silky's faces.

Micah halted. Disgust and haughtiness flashed from his eyes connecting with Silky. Silky laughed. Micah was stupid. "Micah Jordan-Wells. Well, if it isn't Newark's Golden Boy. Your payment is just beginning, man."

Micah gave Silky a look that was worthy of a reptile. Silky didn't give a damn—he kept his focus on Micah. "You captured me, my man. But you ain't captured all that there is. All that there is will capture you, Micah. That's word."

Silky had Micah's attention now. "Thy will be done. The flames of fire will engulf you, Micah. You will burn!"

A shiver raced through Micah's body at Silky's words. He rushed across the room toward Silky. His features were twisted and contorted. Silky's words had touched his core.

He stopped in front of Silky and the police guards. "You're scum, Stokes. Like what's on the bottom of my shoe." Micah removed his Italian-leather shoe. He rubbed the bottom of it in Silky's face leaving a trail of dust on his cheek.

Silky didn't even flinch. He just smiled. Micah saw a flash. Behind the depths of Silky's eyes lay something sinister.

"It don't make no never mind Micah Jordan-Wells. You ain't gonna escape, my brother. You'll be caught up in the rapture. You know about that. Don't you?" Silky's eyes became mere slits. Then he opened them. A glaze-filled trance covered his pupils.

His gaze bored into Micah putting a lock on his soul. "You don't even know who you are. Your world as you know it ain't no more, Micah. Poof." Silky laughed. "Smoke and mirrors, my man. Mirrors and smoke." Silky bowed his head paying homage. He mocked Micah.

The windows of Micah's eyes flickered. Hot electricity crackled in the air. Silky faltered, confused by what he saw. The bowels of his being flipped, opened and flushed. White-hot pain seared his insides.

Silky howled a wolf-keening laugh. Realizing too late that he had been played. Then he burst into flames before Micah's eyes. The courtroom filled with the sight and acrid odor of Silky's burning flesh. His howling turned to shrieks of pain and dark torture.

There was one liquid motion of body movement as the media and most of the spectators rushed out of the doors. Some just stared in rapt fascination at the unfolding evil taking place before their eyes.

Pure pandemonium broke loose. Silky, who had been torched into a human fireball, weaved to the left and then to the right. He finally fell to the floor, a smoldering blanket of flames. Not one person moved to help put out the flames.

Nugent stood in a semi-state of shock. Wolfgang shouted, "We've got to get this under control."

Micah looked at the flaming Silky and said, "Nugent, call the medical examiner and tell him to get here quick. We need some answers." Wolfgang ran down the aisle with Micah right behind him.

Out on the courtyard steps, Wolfgang stepped into his element. This was his city. He'd be damned if any criminal would usurp him. Even one who had suddenly burst into flames.

Wolfgang, composed as a picture of calm assurance, stepped before the public. He waved his hands at the press to garner their attention.

Meanwhile, police vehicles and fire trucks screamed in the distance. A rookie police officer handed Wolfgang a bullhorn.

"Listen to me," Wolfgang said, "David Edward Stokes, also known as Silky, has burst into flames. Medical assistance is on the way. After we have examined Mr. Stokes we will have more information."

Wolfgang handed the bullhorn back to the officer. He turned his back on the media and made his way through the crowd as they shouted out unanswered questions. Micah followed him. He made no comment at all.

Derrick Holt, who had kicked off the media circus with Micah before the start of the penalty trial leaped forward from the crowd. "What the hell happened, Wolfgang?" Unknowingly, he was parroting Wolfgang's exact thoughts.

"Was Silky affiliated with the occult? Come on, the people of Newark have a right to know. He burst into flames. What gives?"

Wolfgang stopped in midstride. He turned to stare at Derrick. "That's all I have for now." He pushed his way through the crowd.

Wolfgang's statement only heightened the air of edginess. But their shouted out questions went unanswered. The policemen and firemen moved in to break up the crowd and maintain order.

Derrick stared thoughtfully at Wolfgang's departing back.

Micah turned back to look at Derrick. They waged a silent eye battle, metamorphosing into the invisible line between the police and the press.

Derrick was no match for Micah. So he backed off breaking the intense eye contact.

Derrick stuck a toothpick in his mouth. Frantically he gnawed at the tip of it. Ever since he stopped smoking the toothpick was a must. It kept him sane.

Never mind Wolfgang and Micah for now he decided. They were going to come face-to-face with his master research. Then he'd see what they had to say.

Hell, what did they think he was? Crazy? People didn't just burst into flames. "What's done in the dark, always comes to the light," Derrick muttered under his breath as he made his way through the crowd. He headed to his office.

Micah entered the now-empty courtroom ahead of Wolfgang and Nugent to discover Silky had left him a message. Seared into the wall behind the judge's bench was a melted down charcoal warning. "Your chains can't hold me! And your fire can't destroy me!"

Micah looked over at the defense table where Silky had been seated to find the shackles and chains that had held him sitting in the seat. Impossible. He walked over and picked them up. To his surprise, they were cold to the touch. They didn't have a scorch mark on them.

When he looked down at Silky's smoldering ashes he found that Silky had also left him a single mark by which he was to be remembered. The ashes had been arranged in the form of an "X." A thin waft of smoke trickled up from the ashes that used to be Silky.

When Wolfgang and Nugent entered the courtroom they saw none of what Micah had witnessed.

Chapter 6

Derrick stood at his desk in the cluttered, crowded, noisy newsroom of the *Star-Ledger* newspaper. Telephones rang. Pagers were going off. The constant click-clacking of computer keys were in rhyme and rhythm. They all provided the familiar background music of his world.

His desk was a study in organized messiness. Paper created the order of his world. Though it may not look like it, he knew where every scrap of paper and every scribbled note lay.

Chris White, a fellow reporter, spotted him. He headed straight over to his desk. "Man, you have got to be kidding me. I know David Stokes didn't blow up in the court today. Right?" Chris waited for Derrick's answer.

Derrick leaned over close to Chris's ear and said, "He did! Silky burst into flames! He just spontaneously combusted! Just like that!" Derrick snapped his fingers.

"Like he was on a timer. You had to be there, Chris. It was really weird. I mean like tenth-degree weird. Something ain't right."

Derrick sat down heavily in his chair. Chris perched on the edge of Derrick's desk.

Chris looked at Derrick. "All right, run it down for me."

Derrick exhaled. "There was a- a- a sort of black chemistry in the air. Between Micah Jordan-Wells and Silky. It was like electricity crackling. I mean you couldn't see it but you could definitely feel it. Know what I mean? Then just like that. Boom. Silky exploded. Turned into a flaming wonder. When's the last time you've seen a man just burst into flames?"

Chris raised an eyebrow but didn't speak. Derrick jerked open his side drawer. He took out a new toothpick. He spit the old one into the trash.

The toothpick habit annoyed Chris, but he knew better than to comment. Derrick was a reformed smoker.

Finally, laughing, Chris said, "Okay. I haven't seen anyone burst into flames. But, don't go getting all superstitious on me. This is news, not fantasy. Let a brother give you a one up. You'd be wise to treat it as news." Chris knew how Derrick's mind operated. He knew Derrick was in overdrive.

"There are a few documented cases in the United States regarding spontaneous human combustion. Things happen, Derrick. Some things are more easily explained than others are. That's all. Your job is to unearth the facts. You can't give in to runaway suspicions. If a man explodes there must be a reason why."

Derrick was not moved by Chris's little speech. He didn't like the feel of this one. Jitters ran up and down his spine. He felt like someone was walking over his grave. Making up his mind he said, "The Prince of Darkness just made a visit to Newark."

Chris sighed. "Have you seen him personally?"

Derrick leaned back in his chair. "Hell, yeah. Problem is, I'm just not sure whose face he was wearing."

Chris frowned.

Derrick's eyes remained on Chris's face. Then he spun around and booted up his computer. He typed in the headline; "Micah Jordan-Wells Slays Another of Newark's Dragons."

Chapter 7

Micah stood outside of Evelyn's gabled Victorian house. When he was a kid the house used to give him the creeps, with its multitude of rooms, creaking floors and whistling windows. Not to mention the images that seemed to float around at their own will.

He'd seen them hovering around in hallways. They also lingered in remote corners of the house. But, when he told his mother she always dismissed it as his overactive imagination. He'd wondered then and sometimes he still wondered now.

Reverend Jackson hadn't been any better at trying to explain his flights of fantasy to him. Micah had found the reverend's explanations even more disturbing because it was almost as if he himself didn't quite believe what he was telling Micah.

He used to wish he had someone to really share the haunting feelings with, as well as the burdens of his mother.

It was hard to believe that in the years she had lived in the house, his mother hadn't seen the weeping old woman. The one with the outstretched arms that she held out to him, as tears streamed down her face. Her hair flew out behind her as though a great wind were blowing it. Always she was dressed in a flannel white nightgown with a high collar.

Whenever Micah saw her it was always the same old thing. She reached out her arms to him weeping in sorrow. He had nicknamed her the "Weeping Willow" when he was a kid. Strangely enough he hadn't seen her since he was grown.

He wished he hadn't started on this train of thought because all it did was increase his frustration regarding his mother. As he stood looking at the gabled house, the memories had flooded him.

He also felt something else. He shivered. He looked up to see the vines on one of the trees blowing in the wind. There was no wind. None of the branches or leaves on the other trees was blowing.

The vines turned to claws, reaching for him. Micah shook himself. He was a grown man now. Not a kid. He wouldn't stand for this. He blinked and the image disappeared.

Micah blew out a harsh breath. He didn't know why Evelyn insisted on living in this house. He wished she would move to something lighter and brighter, maybe a nice town house.

Although he respected his heritage and the inheritance of the house, it carried a certain weight. Its historical value aside, he preferred to leave the ghosts of the past as well as his ancestors in the past. But Evelyn insisted on keeping them alive by not relinquishing the old Victorian.

Finally, he glided to the porch and stuck his key in the lock. Entering the foyer Micah called out, "Ma, hey Ma, where are you?"

Evelyn was standing in the kitchen pouring a cup of coffee. Upon hearing Micah's voice she quickly laced her coffee with Chivas Regal.

Evelyn Jordan-Wells was now an agoraphobic, renowned novelist writing under the pseudonym of Blaine Upshaw. "I'm in the kitchen Micah," she yelled.

Micah passed through the parlor on his way to the kitchen and two items on Evelyn's writing table caught his eye.

He spotted the daily newspaper with its blaring headline. "Micah Jordan-Wells Slays Another of Newark's Dragons." A picture of Micah staring at a flaming Silky exploded from the front page. Micah looked at it. Then he tossed the paper into the wastepaper basket.

Next he picked up the Advanced Reading Copy of Evelyn's newest novel, *In the Garden of Eden*. Micah stared at the novel without opening it and Evelyn walked into the parlor, observing his keen interest in the book.

"Micah, what's keeping you?" she asked.

Micah held up the novel. "Is this the latest and greatest?"

Evelyn tilted her head watching Micah. She bit her bottom lip, a bad habit she had developed over the years and replied, "Yes. Yes, it is."

Micah finally turned to look at her and said, "It's a strange title."

Evelyn walked over and touched Micah's arm while looking up at him gently. "It's gothic romance, Micah. The concept is derived from the pureness of the experience between the first man and woman."

Micah looked at her cynically. "It wasn't all pureness, lady. There was a serpent in that garden."

Evelyn hesitated her eyes growing serious. "As there is in every garden. You are so cynical at times, Micah."

Micah gave her his most long-suffering look. The one he reserved for her whenever she said things like that. "It's what's kept me alive so far."

Evelyn pulled a wry smile. "Touché, Micah. Touché."

She reached into the wastepaper basket retrieving the newspaper. "I see you've been making more headlines of your own. Slaying dragons and all that."

Micah replied, "Yeah, I make it happen and one day the hunters are the hunted and the slayers are the slain."

Unknowingly he had touched a raw nerve in Evelyn. She snapped at him. "Do not be dark with me, Micah."

She laid the newspaper back on her writing desk. Micah was immediately apologetic. "I'm sorry, Ma. I've got a lot on my mind. Listen, I just came by to see if you needed anything."

He paused for a moment, looking at her pointedly. "I wanted to take you for a walk."

A flash of naked fear crossed Evelyn's face. She hyperventilated. Micah was accustomed to these attacks so he put an arm around her shoulders.

"You know I can't go for a walk, Micah," Evelyn's raspy voice was almost a whisper.

A tremor passed through her body. Her breathing was harsh and loud. Somewhere in the background a whistling wind floated through the house. A symphony of screeching voices rode through the room on an invisible blanket of sound that only Evelyn could hear.

Gently, Micah guided her to a chair. He eased her down on the chair and patted one of her hands soothingly. "Ma, one day soon, you're going to have to go outside. There is nothing to be afraid of."

Evelyn moaned. She shook her head from side to side. She panted, "No, Micah. Never. I just can't. I know it is just an illness . . ." She couldn't finish her sentence. Her eyes were framed photographs of dismay.

Micah had consulted every expert psychiatrist, as well as every psychologist available. They had all been to this house at one time or another. The bottom line was that Evelyn had to overcome her fears by facing them. But she was incapacitated and could not bring herself to do so.

Evelyn hadn't ever left the house in all the years that he had been alive. Micah's shoulders slumped from the tragedy of it all.

No psychiatrist or psychologist had ever been able to determine the source of Evelyn's fear. All they knew was that prior to Micah's birth, she had stopped going outside. She had not stepped out of the house since. So much for experts.

Micah stared at his mother. His eyes held a questioning look. He decided to let it go. Every time they had this conversation of her going outside, it ended exactly the same way.

He couldn't bear to see her in pain. The issue of her going outside always produced that pain, the sudden fear. He wondered once again at the source of it and then backed away as he drew the usual blank.

He watched Evelyn retreat into that special place of hers. Where warm and embracing arms reached out to comfort her.

Micah didn't know. He could never understand. How could he possibly ever, ever understand? Nor could she jeopardize him for any reason. No. No, there was just no way. She watched Micah's face slowly fade away from her world.

Evelyn sought peace, in that corner of her mind that had been helping her for more than thirty years.

Micah brushed long, dark locks of hair peppered with gray, back from her brow, knowing and accepting she was beyond his reach for the moment.

Chapter 8

That night, Micah lay in his bedroom with his girlfriend, Raven Oliver. Raven was the owner of a specialty boutique shop in Newark. She was also a model in New York City. She had a flair for fashion that overflowed into her life. It made her a vibrant individual. Style and class were stamped all over her.

She was a tall, svelte, young woman with an athletic body, caramel-colored skin and soulful-looking brown eyes, which at times appeared too large for her face.

It was exactly this look that had helped her to grace the covers of some fine magazines. Raven's eyes were a startling brown with flecks of gold. When she stared out from a magazine cover, all you could see were those eyes and the fine high cheekbones accentuating her face.

She was also hell on a runway. When she strutted down the aisle, generally every eye and camera was fastened on her.

Raven had known Micah was meant for her from the start. Though there were times when Micah's mystique baffled her. Sometimes he seemed so near and yet so far away. But there was no denying that the impact of a look from Micah sent quivers up and down her spine. With a single look he had laid claim to her heart. She was locked in solid.

* * *

Micah and Raven lay on a thick rug on the floor of his bedroom watching the flames leap and crackle from the fireplace. Candles were burning around the room. Micah was finally getting some much-needed relaxation.

As Micah relaxed, the one who never slept watched his every move from in between the beams of his walls. As he watched intently, he reduced Micah to nothing but an aura, removing the physicality of the man that Micah was. He did not like what he saw. Still, he continued to watch.

Raven traced Micah's hairline softly with one finger. Slow, tantalizing music reverberated from giant surround-sound speakers. A silver bucket filled with ice held a bottle of Möet. Raven leaned over for a long lingering kiss.

She pulled back to look at Micah. "Why don't you take a break, Micah? Get away from the demons of the streets. Let's go away. It's been so long since we've been out of Newark."

Suddenly one of the candles blew out. Micah gave it a strange look. He reached over and relit it. Raven looked around the room. There was no draft.

Returning to the conversation Micah said, "We'll go. Soon. How's the house hunting going? Have you seen anything I'd want to be king of the castle in?"

Raven smiled. She was aware of Micah's penchant for changing difficult subjects. He was definitely sidestepping her now. "No. I haven't yet seen home and hearth. I'm still looking."

Micah poured some champagne in their glasses. He looked tenderly at Raven. "Soon. I promise. Soon. Come on, let's dance."

He pulled Raven to her feet, pulling her into a tight embrace. Slowly they twined their bodies, content to just hold each other.

Raven nibbled on Micah's ear. "If you keep this up I might forgive you for not giving me a definite answer."

Micah laughed. "I'm giving you candlelight, firelight, champagne and love. What more do you want?"

Raven looked up at him wistfully. "That's easy. I want you Micah, all of you. And when the time comes, a baby. I'd name him Micah Jordan-Wells Jr. It has a nice ring to it. Doesn't it?"

The distinct cry of a baby rang out at the mention of her words. Both of them stopped in their tracks. "Was that you?" Raven said.

She had heard the rumors of Micah's ventriloquist days in the police academy. Back when he had thought it was funny to imitate the voices of different criminals.

"It wasn't me." The hair stood up on his arms. He released Raven, looking around the room. He went to the window and looked out. There was nothing.

The cry rang out once again.

Raven grabbed her midsection as a sharp, knifelike pain stabbed through her stomach muscles. Upon hearing the cry something in her womb had jumped. It knocked the breath out of her. In an instant it was gone.

"Micah. Something's going on."

"Nothing's going on. Forget it, Raven." He didn't want her getting spooked, but he definitely didn't like the happenings. "Maybe we just had too much champagne." They both looked at the barely touched bottle.

"Just forget about it." Micah lay down on the rug. "Come over here." Raven shrugged off the feeling. She didn't want the night to be ruined by what probably amounted to some stranger's baby crying. But what about the stomach pains? She sighed, pushing the thought from her mind.

Micah laughed. "I never figured you for the barefoot and pregnant type."

Raven gave him an indignant look. "If it's draped in contemporary dignity I could be. Yes."

They both giggled, releasing the tension. "I love you Raven. One day you're going to have it all. I'm going to see to that. Just give it a little more time. Okay?"

Raven nodded her surrender. She pulled Micah's face to hers for the sweetness of his kiss.

"Besides, I need time to gather a little more change so I can buy you that big rock I've been thinking of."

Raven pushed Micah back against the rug. She grinned. "Just how big of a rock are we talking about here?"

Micah shook his head not giving an inch. "It's a man's prerogative. I'll never tell. Big enough so your girlfriends don't miss it."

Raven laughed. "You are such an ego-tripper."

"You know you love it."

"Yeah. I do. Give me the rock!"

Micah smiled. The telephone rang. A look of annoyance flashed across Raven's face. "Micah do not answer it. Please."

Micah sat up. "I have to. You know that."

"No, you don't."

He winked at Raven but she would not be placated. She turned her head away, pouting like a petulant child.

The telephone continued to ring. He lifted the receiver. "Micah Jordan-Wells here."

He listened intently to the voice on the line. A closed mask instantly settled itself over Micah's features.

As Raven watched an enigmatic energy seeped from Micah's pores. It bounced off the walls in the room. She watched in a state of disbelief as Micah slammed the phone down. He raced from the room without a second thought.

From in between the beams of the walls Quentin gave a satisfied smile. With that he was gone.

Raven ran after Micah. When she caught up with him, she wheeled him around to face her. "Where are you going? Come on, Micah. Not tonight. All I ever do is wait for you. I'm tired of waiting. We never have any time together. It's always the job. You have to make some time for you and me. We need a life."

Micah briefly caught her face between his hands. "And we'll have one. I promise. But right now I have to go. I'm sorry Raven. I'll make it up to you." He dropped a distracted kiss on her cheek. Before she could say another word, he was gone.

Tears of frustration rolled down Raven's cheeks. She went into the bedroom. Looking at the bottle of champagne, she picked it up. Angry frustration sizzled through her body. She hurled the champagne into the fireplace.

She was always sitting on eternal wait for Micah. She was always worried about him. She was scared that one day he wouldn't return. No matter what she said to him she knew she was not getting through. He was obsessed with chasing monsters.

Raven went home to her own apartment. Her roommate and business partner in the boutique, Brandi, looked up from the television as Raven walked through the door.

One look at Raven's face and Brandi knew the title of this song. "Cancelled again, huh? When are you going to get a life, Raven, and stop waiting for the crumbs from Micah's life?"

Raven turned on Brandi in white-hot fury. "Mind your own damn business, Brandi. Micah is my business. I'll wait for him as long as I damned well please. Okay? For once, just mind your own business."

Raven walked into her bedroom. She slammed the door so hard the walls shook.

Brandi turned back to the TV and her bowl of popcorn. "Sister girl's got a bad case," she uttered to the empty room.

Chapter 9

Micah careened through the dark Newark streets to the homicide department. He screeched into a parking space. Jumping out of the car he left the door wide open. He raced up the steps. Just as he reached the door, Nugent opened it.

"Micah, this one is really bad. Wolfgang is waiting for you." Nugent hurried to keep pace with Micah as he ran to Wolfgang's office.

As they passed through the corridors, Micah could see the detectives and police officers were in high gear. A storm was definitely brewing.

Several officers looked up as Micah ran by with Nugent at his heels. Reaching Wolfgang's office, he pushed open the door without waiting for an invitation.

The big man was standing and waiting to greet him. Immediately upon Micah's entrance, Wolfgang said, "I'm sorry about interrupting your evening, Micah, but I need you on this."

Wolfgang ran a weary hand through his hair.

Micah waved the statement away irritably. "Forget it, Wolfgang. What's up?"

Nugent and Wolfgang exchanged looks. The air bristled with an electric current. Micah placed one hand on Wolfgang's desk and the other on his hip, exuding arrogance and anger in one swift move. "What's going down?"

Wolfgang walked over to the window. He looked out over the city of Newark. He had decided to bring Micah to the office rather than the crime scene so he could brief him and they could ride together to the scene.

Micah waited. Nugent watched them both through half-closed eyes.

"We need to take a ride. Someone is killing our children."

A hollow pain ripped through Micah's gut. "Then let's go."

Micah, Wolfgang, and Nugent sped to the crime scene on Clinton Avenue. They pulled into the driveway just beyond where the police had cordoned off the scene. The area was crowded with policemen. Micah jumped out before the car came to a halt.

He walked up to Sidney Bowden, the charge officer. "Nobody touched anything here. Right?"

Sidney shook his head. "No one has touched a thing, sir. We've been waiting for you. Once you're done, we'll go to work." Micah nodded his approval.

Sidney pointed to a nearby Dumpster. "In there," he said. Micah gave him a look that could fry bacon. Then he walked over to the Dumpster. A vivid red thick substance was splattered across the Dumpster. It read "'X' was here." Micah blinked.

He climbed a small plastic-covered step stool that had been placed near the Dumpster. He turned around and Nugent handed him latex gloves before he could ask the question. Micah nodded his thanks.

He leaned over and peered into the Dumpster. An awful evil stared back at him. Micah was unprepared for what he saw. The nude body of a six-year-old boy lay in the Dumpster. The child lay in his own urine and feces. The boy's body was drenched in blood. The carving of an "X" had split open the middle of his chest.

His eyes stared at the twilight of the sky. They were filmed over with a glaze that only enhanced the petrified look in them.

Rigid eternity glared at Micah. The child's last expression was one of scathing, horrid fear. The fear was so cloying that even after death it hung in the air. Micah could feel it.

The nails in the child's body were rusty, ragged and much too large for the size of the child's hands and legs. They had torn and ripped the skin, leaving a trail of ragged, jagged skin, ripped and torn with blood trailing out.

A foamy, white, creamy substance streamed from the boy's lips. The child's mouth was thrown open as though a desperate plea were trying to escape it and it had gotten strangled in the creamy substance.

Micah had dealt with more homicides than he could count during his career. Some were of a caliber that he would never forget. This homicide carried a level of its own. It was a clear breach. Micah was staring at depravity at its highest level. He choked back the bile that rose in his throat.

One hand stroked his chin. His eyes were glued to the contents inside the Dumpster. He opened his mouth to speak, but discovered that only air hissed out; no words had come forth.

And then he saw her from the corner of his eye. Weeping Willow. She was standing at the rim of the garbage Dumpster; her arms were outstretched reaching out to him. Tears streamed in a steady cascade down her cheeks.

Her hair blew out behind her. She looked down on the child in the garbage can. When her eyes met Micah's they were filled with despair. Her tears continued to flow.

Micah felt a cold draft. He was chilled to the bone. Weeping Willow hadn't uttered a single word. She never did. As Micah watched, she disappeared into the mist of the night.

He knew it was useless to ask if anyone else had seen her. If they had they would have spoken because she had no right to be inside the crime scene.

Micah hadn't seen her since his eighteenth birthday. Now, here she was back again. To make matters worse, a child lay in front of him, split open to the gills, with the same mark that continually haunted him.

He turned to look at Wolfgang and Nugent. He tried again to form the words. They finally came out of his mouth sounding short and clipped. "The boy looks to be about six years old. He's been sliced. An 'X' is branded into his forehead."

Micah leaned over the boy's body. He read the blood-splattered note that was nailed in his neck. The note was printed in the flowing script of a computer: "What Is The Tie That Binds?"

Micah climbed down from the Dumpster. He mentally ordered

his legs to follow his commands because suddenly his legs were operating like jelly. He was shaky and weak, as a tremor rode through his arms and legs.

There were few things in life that had ever truly riled Micah. Nothing had ever rendered him immobile. But seeing this slaughtered child, thrown away like so much garbage was one of them.

Only years of discipline, training, and professionalism held back the fit that was brewing just below his surface. He wanted to hurt somebody.

Micah yelled to Sidney, "Get this boy out of the garbage and be careful with him. I need to know if there has been any sexual contact." Micah walked away from the scene to get into the car.

Wolfgang pushed him a step farther into the dark abyss he was about to enter. "There's another one. They're holding the scene on Hawthorne Avenue for us."

Micah didn't respond. He slid into the passenger seat. They raced off to the next scene.

When Micah, Wolfgang, and Nugent walked in the door on Hawthorne Avenue they were immediately assaulted with the horrific nature that left no respect for human life.

Splashed haphazardly in blood across the walls was the question, "What Is The Tie That Binds?" The sign of the "X" beckoned. "'X' was here" completed the message.

Micah crossed the room to a small bundle that lay on the floor. He looked down, observing the same age and pattern as that of the boy on Clinton Avenue. This time there was no Weeping Willow.

Micah's mind raced, reviewing the pattern of the killer. Creating a profile for him. Thinking out loud, he said, "These murders have Silky's signature on them. We might be dealing with a copycat."

A scream shattered and penetrated the insulated world inside the apartment. Nakisha Thompson stood in the doorway. She was the mother of the six-year-old victim.

She stared at the body of her son on the floor. A high-pitched wail flew from her lips, "Rasheem! Oh my God! Rasheem! That's my baby. Rasheem, get up. Rasheem! Get up baby, get up now!"

Nakisha stepped forward. The shock etched on her face turned it into a porcelain vision. She trembled. Then she collapsed. One of the uniformed policemen caught her as she fell. She slumped in his arms.

Micah stared at the boy's mother. Violent rage swept through him at her pain. His heart thumped. But he managed to hold himself in rigid control.

A sudden movement outside the window caught Micah's eye. There was someone out on the fire escape. His face was painted white. His eyes were circled in red and black paint. So was his nose. His head was covered in a black skullcap. He was totally outfitted in black. And he was peering in the window.

"What the—? Is that a mime?" Micah was bugging. Hell no. Who the hell was outside on the fire escape of his murder scene? What the hell? Did they think this was some kind of game?

The face disappeared from the window as Micah approached. Momentarily it appeared again. The mime pulled long eyes and a sad face at Micah.

That was it. Micah lunged in the direction of the windowsill. He saw the mime's black-clad legs race past the window.

He shot a quick glance at Nugent. "I want him. Block off everything in the area, including the sewers."

Nugent barked orders at the officers in the room. Micah leaped out the window onto the fire escape in time to see the mime jump off the bottom of the fire escape. He followed at a rapid speed. The chase was on.

The mime whizzed through alleyways knocking over everything in his way. Micah was right on his heels.

He raced ahead only to find a solid wall of cement blocking his path. He had run into a dead end.

He looked around, wildly searching for an out. Finding no escape, he frantically turned to face the wrath that was Micah Jordan-Wells.

He looked at Micah's enraged features. The gun was pointed at his forehead. "Halt! Don't move!" Micah shouted. He saw Micah's lips moving. He was shouting at him. But, he couldn't hear a word Micah said.

A sound like that of a wounded animal rose out of the mime's lips. He shrank to the wall. He raised his hands in the air. He looked sadly at Micah. Tears spilled out from his painted eyes.

Chapter 10

Later that night in the interrogation room of the homicide department, Micah stood watching the mime. He was sitting forlornly in a chair. He sipped nervously from a glass of water.

The door burst open. Nugent raced up to Micah with the investigative information. "Micah, this is Ronnie Schaefer. He is the Thompson boy's neighbor."

Micah didn't budge or remove his gaze from Ronnie. Nugent continued. "Nakisha Thompson confirmed his identity. He's a deaf mute, Micah. He can't hear or speak. Ronnie Schaefer is nineteen years old. He's a friend of Rasheem and Nakisha's. He's dressed as a mime for a neighborhood Halloween party. We've checked. Everything is in order. There's no way he committed the murder."

Micah continued to watch Ronnie while processing Nugent's information. "He saw the murderer. He knows who he is. He knows who killed Rasheem Thompson. He's not leaving until I know who killed Rasheem."

Nugent sputtered, "Micah, even the babysitter doesn't know . . . she—"

Micah brusquely cut Nugent off. "I said he knows. I can see it in his eyes. Get me an interpreter and the police sketch artist."

Micah didn't care about the distraught babysitter, who had carelessly left a six-year-old child alone in the apartment, while she flirted with her boyfriend in front of the building. She couldn't provide a clue to this insanity. She'd walked back into the apartment to find the child had been slaughtered in her absence. On Halloween night, like a scene from some grotesque movie.

Ronnie Schaefer was a different story. He had seen the killer. There was no doubt. Micah knew he had seen him. How to carefully craft it out of him was the only question. The reflection of something haunting and terror-stricken was mirrored in the pools of Ronnie Schaefer's eyes.

Ronnie looked at Micah who never took his eyes off of him. He suddenly jumped up from his seat. He signed wildly at Nugent. He ran up to Nugent and grabbed him desperately.

He appeared to want to be away from Micah. He gestured wildly at Nugent. His eyes begged Nugent to understand.

Nugent looked at Micah—whom he knew was seething. Micah was about to blow. He glanced briefly at Ronnie Schaefer who definitely was not helping matters and said, "Why don't you take a break man. Let me try. Just take a break for a minute. Okay?"

Micah stalked to the door without another word. He flung it open leaving the room. He slammed it shut behind him. He should not have. On the other side of the door, the dead boy who had been lying in the Dumpster the last time Micah had seen him was walking through the hall. He turned his head to look at Micah.

A sharp gasp of air flew upwards from Micah's insides. A loud voice boomed through the hall saying, "Dead boy walking. Dead boy walking."

The child suddenly stopped walking. He turned to face Micah, a full frontal impact. Micah stood stock-still. A force blew the child against the wall. His body was turned upside down. Ragged nails flew into every inch of his body, nailing him to the wall.

Blood literally flew out of the body of the splayed child. A multitude of the ragged nails carved the boy's flesh into the illustration of an "X." The "X" turned into a flaming inferno before Micah's eyes. And then, there was laughter.

Micah leaned over, his body racked with dry heaves. He looked up to discover the entire hallway was deserted. He watched in stupefied repulsion as the "X" erased itself from the wall. All traces of what he'd seen had vanished.

Micah grabbed his head as pain of a terrific magnitude tore through his brain and squeezed tight.

One hour later, having composed himself, Micah was on the other side of the glass looking into the interrogation room. His icy gaze took in the transpiring scene. Nugent, Ronnie Schaefer, the interpreter and the police sketch artist were all there. Wolfgang stood silently beside Micah, also watching the events unfold.

Inside the interrogation room, Nugent was setting the final stage. "Ask him if he's sure the person he described to us is the murderer," he said to the interpreter.

The interpreter signed the question. Ronnie signed back. His lips moved. The interpreter answered, "He says, absolutely."

Unexpectedly, Ronnie jumped up. He acted out details of the murder. He threw his arms out spread-eagle in the air.

Wails of anguish and fear emanated from him just as they had emanated from the murdered boy before the life left his body.

The police sketch artist exchanged a strange look with the interpreter.

Nugent lost his cool. He looked at the police sketch artist and said, "Let me see the sketch."

Outside the interrogation room Micah pressed his nose against the glass. The moment was here. He was going to see the face of the killer.

This was all Micah needed. The sight would put him inside the mind and body of the killer. It was for him a visual manifestation in the flesh. He could see the murder as it had taken place. Once there the killer would belong to him. He would breathe the same air. Hear his thoughts. He would witness his actions. Then he would hunt him down like the dog he was.

Micah had a keen sense of telepathy, one that he had never discussed with anyone. More than once he had walked inside the mind of a killer and brought him to justice. More than once he had experienced the rage of a maniac flowing through his veins. He couldn't explain it. It was just something that he did.

Inside the interrogation room the police sketch artist handed Nugent the sketch. Nugent looked down at it. Pure shock volleyed with disbelief for position across his numb features.

He stared dumbfounded at the interpreter and the police sketch artist. Finally, his look turned to one of absolute puzzlement as it settled on Ronnie Schaefer.

Micah lost his patience. He stormed into the interrogation room. His disruptive entrance startled everyone in the room, knocking them off balance.

Micah didn't care. He strolled arrogantly up to Nugent. "Give me the sketch, Nugent. I want to see the maniac's face."

Micah snatched the sketch from Nugent's numb fingers, while Wolfgang, who had entered the room behind him, tried to ascertain what the hell was actually going on in the room. The vibe was off-kilter. Wolfgang didn't like interrogations that were off-kilter.

Micah looked down at the sketch. He could have been looking in the mirror.

His eyes grew wide in shocked anger as well as unmistakable amazement. Bile rose in his throat. Micah spat on the floor directly at the feet of Ronnie Schaefer.

His gaze landed on Ronnie. It practically sucked him into a vortex. Ronnie took a step back as though he'd been slapped.

Finally, Micah's gaze found Nugent. Ronnie gestured wildly and the interpreter spoke, "Ronnie Schaefer says that Micah Jordan-Wells is the man he saw commit the murder."

An appalling silence gripped the room. Only the harsh sound of Ronnie's breathing penetrated the reign of silence that had settled like a dark cloud in the room.

Wolfgang was the first to recover. He snatched the sketch from Micah's stiff fingers. "That's ridiculous. What the hell is going on here? I'm not in the mood to play games with this boy. I'll lock his ass up for eternity."

Wolfgang turned to Nugent, jumping down his throat. Icy scorn laced his voice. "Get me some real answers. Ronnie Schaefer doesn't move for the next seventy-two hours. I don't give a damn if the attorney general is going to represent him. Am I clear?"

Nugent nodded. He hadn't quite found his voice yet. Ronnie Schaefer had delivered a punch that had sucked all the available air from his body.

Wolfgang stalked to the door. He stopped to look back at those in the room. His eyes glittered in their anger. "I swear, if one word of what was said in this room tonight leaks out, Micah and I will be the only ones working here. And I guarantee you'll never work in law enforcement again. Do I make myself clear?" Quickly, all heads except Ronnie Schaefer's nodded.

Wolfgang shook his head to clear it from the madness that was floating around in it. "Micah, check your closets, man. It looks like you have some powerful enemies that are coming out to play."

Micah didn't respond. Wolfgang left the room, banging the door shut behind him.

Micah Jordan-Wells looked down at the floor. He stared at the molten "X" that appeared before his eyes. It beckoned to him. Drawing him closer to his existence. Everyone else in the room had ceased to be.

Chapter II

Shaughn Braswell sat in the midst of a silver-and-chrome living room. He admired himself in all angles of the mirrored room.

Sofas and tables decorated the room. In the middle of the room sat a large table covered with sculpting tools. Every tool was in its place. The room was fastidiously clean. The high ceilings sported whitewashed beams.

Shaughn Braswell was tall and athletic. He had long dreadlocks pulled back in a ponytail. His looks were every bit of the handsome yet rugged rogue. His skin resembled porcelain. He had long lashes that fluttered over eyes that reflected an eerie emptiness. Sometimes they lit up with the miracle of creation.

His long handsome fingers were made to sculpt, to mold, and create. It was his gift.

Shaughn's face reflected intense concentration. He had just put the finishing touches on a sculpture. This was one of his favorite pastimes.

He stroked his long goatee. It was perfectly trimmed, as were his mustache and sideburns. Restlessly he stared at the front page of Newark's *Star-Ledger* newspaper.

Shaughn was a man that exuded a dangerously dark air. He had a you-don't-want-to-mess-with-me vibe. In the circle he ran in, he was not a man to be toyed with.

Next to the newspaper sat his recently finished, lavishly appointed, beautifully sculptured headpiece of Micah Jordan-Wells. He was mesmerized by the image that was Micah. He could feel him, taste him and touch him. The depths of his eyes were alive, alive at the second and third levels.

A shattering ring interrupted Shaughn. It pulled him out of his reverie. He picked up the phone. "We are perfectly positioned," he said into the phone.

He listened. Then nodded his head in satisfaction. "Good. Let the games begin."

He salivated at the thought of what was to come. "Micah. Micah Jordan-Wells. Welcome to my world, little man. Welcome to my world."

Chapter 12

It was early morning in downtown Newark. Newark was a city that had in many ways been left behind. Since the riots of the '60s there was very little corporate commerce in the city. It was also a ghost of the city it used to be. The streets were strewn with vendors or street merchants who peddled their wares.

On this morning, the streets were brimming with those who were setting up for the day's business. Small shops and restaurants were dishing out the morning's coffee and pastry. The dealmakers were on the streets ready to get paid.

Derrick Holt had been waiting patiently inside the bustling corner coffee shop. As he sipped from his cup of tea he finally spotted Shimmy.

Shimmy was a part of the streets of Newark, a street historian in his own right. He had been on the streets for as long as Derrick could remember. He was also plugged into the word. There was very little that happened in Newark, be it personal, political, or criminal that Shimmy didn't know about.

He was part of a vast network of both criminals and politicians that shared information. He was the grapevine. If anything weird or out of order happened in Newark or on its streets, Shimmy was the man. Trusted in the streets by both the lowly and the mighty, he was a skinny little dude with a big attitude.

Derrick watched him as he set up his wagon of CDs, cassettes and movies. If there was music you couldn't get or find for any reason, then Shimmy was the person you went to. People from as far away as upscale Montclair came into Newark to purchase music from him or to get hard-to-find music, like 12-inch records.

Derrick was tired of waiting, so he drained his cup of tea. He strode purposely up to Shimmy while chewing on his ever-present toothpick.

Shimmy had been watching him. He sighed. Derrick was a major pain in the ass when he wanted something. He didn't know how to leave things alone. Shimmy had erected an entire life of survival on the streets built on this very principle.

On the other hand, Derrick had proved to be useful in some situations for him. He was a researcher. He would provide information when you needed to find out something. He just wished Derrick wasn't such a pest when he needed something. He made him want to swat him like a pesky fly.

"Shimmy, I need some information."

Shimmy continued to set up his wagon. Without turning to Derrick, he said, "About?"

"Silky. I'm doing a piece on him. I know you heard what happened in court. I don't think his whole story came out in court."

Shimmy stopped setting up his cart. He turned to stare at Derrick. "I think you best let that be, my brother. The man is dead. So is his story."

"I don't think so. Was he affiliated with a cult? There's nothing shaking on this street that you don't know about, Shimmy. So I know that you know what the grandstanding Micah did in court didn't cover the whole story. The trial was a joke to Silky."

Shimmy turned his back on Derrick. He selected a CD and popped it into his state-of-the-art boom box. "The man is dead. That's the end of story. Dead is dead. Now leave me alone. It's over, Derrick."

"It ain't over until the fat lady sings and as far as I'm concerned Shimmy, I haven't heard the first note sung yet." Derrick turned and walked down the street.

Across the street, Shaughn Braswell observed the exchange between the two of them with interest.

Chapter 13

Reverend Erwin Jackson sat in his paneled oak library surrounded by his praised collection of Bibles. Books of every sort on the Gospel lined the shelves.

His collection included works of theology and history. He owned Bibles in most of their published languages, covered in every type of binder. He was versed in several languages including Hebrew. His loved tongue was the original language of Ethiopia.

An assortment of tapes of sermons both past and present delivered by pastors known and unknown lined the nooks and crannies in the library. There was also a multitude of commentaries on the Bible. Prayer books as well as documented histories on the life of the apostles after the crucifixion of Jesus Christ completed the awesome collection.

Like some of the men in the Bible, the reverend came from a colorful background. He had been born the son of a prostitute. His father was unknown. He had been abandoned on the steps of a church when he was an infant. His mother had watched over his growth from afar but never introduced herself to him or interfered in his life.

She died as she had lived. She had been found dead in a seedy motel after she turned her last trick. She had tried to place him where she felt he would receive the best. In many ways he had. He had come to know the one power that would shape his life.

One of the priests in the church had decided to shepherd him through his training, and placed him in an orphanage the church was affiliated with. He kept the reverend's mother informed of his progress. Over the years of his childhood, he had sat at the priest's knee, fascinated by the different Bible stories and heroes in the spirit.

His own life had become almost identical to the priest's who helped to raise him. He ministered to abandoned children at the orphanage after he grew up. He tried to lead others in the orphanage to that one guiding light. In his time there, he had seen the good, the bad and the ugly.

Every so often he reaped the fruit of his effort as he had in a young boy over thirty years ago who had sat at his knee hungering for the word. Now that boy was a grown man traveling all over the world. Sharing the life-altering message of Jesus Christ!

Reverend Jackson turned his attention to the front-page picture of Micah Jordan-Wells. He regretted that after all his teaching Micah hadn't followed his footsteps in the ministry.

The boy had been a rapt, as well as a keen, student. He had spent an inordinate amount of time with Micah when he was a boy, teaching him and laying the foundation of the Gospel of Jesus Christ. But Micah had his own mind and agenda. He always had. The old reverend sighed.

Chimes that sounded like the old Negro spiritual "Oh Precious Lord" resounded throughout the house. The reverend rose from his chair. He hadn't been expecting anyone.

When he reached the front door and looked out, he was surprised to see Micah standing on the steps. Micah was admiring the multicolored roses that were springing up around the doorstep.

"Micah. What a pleasure." The two men shook hands. "Come on in." Micah followed the reverend to the library. "Have a seat. Can I get you something to drink?"

"Naw. I'm good. Thanks."

"Well, it's good to see you. How are things in the homicide department?" Micah glanced at the front page of the newspaper the reverend had been reading. Slightly embarrassed, the reverend followed his gaze. Had he known it was Micah at the door he would have put it away. An air of agitation sprung up between them.

"Things are fine Rev," Micah said.

"And your mother?"

Micah smiled. "She's good."

The reverend nodded.

Micah leaned back. He glanced at the old cross hanging on the wall. Pointing to it he said, "What's the cross made out of?"

"Tree bark. There is a claim that they found the original cross that Jesus was crucified on in Labella over in Ethiopia."

Opening his desk drawer, the reverend pulled out a smaller replica of the tree bark cross. There was a warm heat generating from the cross. He'd never felt that before. The reverend looked at Micah thoughtfully. Then he handed him the cross.

Micah didn't touch it. "I can't take that, Rev."

The reverend didn't move his outstretched hand. He gazed into the vibrant pools of Micah's eyes. There was a floating movement in their depths. Micah reached out to take the cross. "Thanks."

The reverend knew deep inside that Micah would need the full power of all it represented. He would need the truth. It wouldn't be much longer. The cross was a simple reminder that sometimes a man's faith and strength must be extraordinary.

He thought about the story of Daniel and the incredible power that God had demonstrated through Daniel for a time, as well as the astounding faith that Daniel had to display in the face of great adversity.

Micah broke into the reverend's thoughts. "You think I need this?" He was surprised at the reverend's gesture for two reasons. First, he knew how rare the cross was and what it meant to him. Second, he hadn't uttered a word of anything out of the ordinary to him. So what had moved him to give him the cross?

"No, Micah. I don't think you need the cross."

Micah frowned.

"I know that you need it, son."

Micah tucked the cross inside his suit jacket pocket. "Then I guess I have what I came for."

The reverend stared into a pair of piercing, damning eyes behind Micah's head. The vision was nothing but the pair of eyes. There was no body attached. The eyes glittered at the reverend. Then they vanished.

"Yes," the reverend said, "I guess you do."

A frown creased Reverend Jackson's brow as his thoughts came to rest on the past of Evelyn Jordan-Wells.

Chapter 14

The following morning the reverend stood facing Evelyn in the foyer of her home. She was somewhat less than happy to see him. He knew it. But it didn't matter.

She had known he would come. She just didn't want to deal with him. She knew it ever since she saw the front-page picture of Micah in the newspaper. Things were spiraling out of control.

She gave the reverend a steady look. "You shouldn't be here, Reverend Jackson."

The reverend didn't mince words with her. "There is darkness being unleashed, Evelyn. A great many years have gone by. Its presence is far-reaching. There are events taking place that you can no longer ignore. We've got to do something."

Evelyn adopted an air of denial and indifference. "I don't know what you're talking about, Reverend."

The reverend lost his patience. He gripped Evelyn by her shoulders. Face up he geared into eye-to-eye contact with her. "Evelyn, you can't ignore this and pretend it's not happening. Your soul will be damned, enough of this hiding. The truth must be told."

Evelyn was rooted to the spot. Mutely she looked at the reverend. She shifted her gaze to the front door behind him. The door banged open.

The reverend released his grip on Evelyn's arms as a force pushed him backward through the foyer. He landed roughly on the front porch.

His face twisted with a stricken look. His eyes glazed over with shock, disbelief, and finally real fear.

"You have a vow of silence, Reverend! Surely you would not consider breaking such a sacred oath!" Evelyn said. Her voice roared like a lion shouting across a valley. The words echoed around him.

The reverend looked at Evelyn. The words had come forth from her lips. But the voice was not hers. Neither were the eyes that looked back at him.

He fingered the cross around his neck, drawing strength from it. Finding his voice he said, "Evelyn please. You've got to listen to me. I . . ." his voice trailed off when he saw the silhouette of Quentin Curry appear behind Evelyn. Quentin was a horrible memory from a not too distant past.

Quentin silenced the reverend with a single look. His eyes glittered like glowing coals from inside the hood that covered his head.

His look held the old man in its grip, suspending him from a very high altitude where the air was very thin. But his feet were still on the ground. Dizziness soared through the reverend's head.

"You have no place here, Reverend."

The reverend breathed deeply. Sudden strength flowed through the reverend's limbs. Air flooded his lungs. "Neither do you."

The old man amused Quentin. He smiled. It had actually been quite a while since anyone had tried to fight him back. He rather enjoyed a good duel every now and then. He decided the reverend would be good sport. "Who is going to keep me out?" he asked as he stared at a trembling Evelyn.

The reverend gazed at Evelyn, who was held in the sharp grip of fear. "Evelyn, you must fight back. Please Evelyn." Not one spoken word left Evelyn's lips. Terror had her rooted to the spot. She had no wellspring she could tap in to. Quentin was stronger than she was. She couldn't beat him.

Revulsion flipped over in the pit of the reverend's stomach. His fierce angry eyes turned to Quentin. "There is one who can keep you out," he said with the faith of Job.

Quentin pulled his hood tighter. His eyes gleamed. "We shall see."

Quentin disappeared from the reverend's line of vision. The door slammed shut in his face disconnecting him from Evelyn.

Reverend Jackson mumbled a prayer under his breath, "Our Father, who art in heaven . . ." Collecting himself he banged on the front door.

"Evelyn, you've got to fight back. You've got to put a stop to this madness. Otherwise it is going to go on and on. Can't you see Evelyn? Evelyn. Please. It's him. I know it's him. You know it's him. Evelyn."

The reverend's pleas and banging went on in vain. Evelyn was unyielding to his requests.

Chapter 15

The following day, Micah was sweating through his ritual morning workout. High-level tension roamed through his body. The cross, made out of tree bark lay around his neck. He had stepped up his workout routine to a maniac level.

Music blared from the hi-tech speakers in the room. Micah dropped to the floor. He matched his push-ups to the rhythm of the beat.

He finished the push-ups, started his stretches. Next came his calisthenics. "Ummm," he moaned as he felt the tension dissolving from his tight muscles.

He jumped on his Torso Track. While he performed the smooth back and forth motion, he emptied his mind. He gave his total focus over to the rhythmic pull of the machine.

He finally rose from the Torso Track, folded it and slid it under the bed. He pulled on his boxing gloves. He pranced. His feet danced lightly over to the heavy double-weight boxing bag. He gave the bag a solid pounding. Twenty, pounding, mind-emptying minutes later Micah was ready to go for his jog.

Tony, a retired policeman who served as doorman as well as security and stock analyst extraordinaire for the building's residents, sat reading the morning newspaper in the front lobby.

Tony looked up from the *Wall Street Journal* as Micah strode to-

ward him. He liked Micah's discipline and agility. The boy had sta-
mina.

Micah had a towel wrapped around his neck. He was outfitted in
his running gear again. Tony watched Micah shadowbox over to
him. He smiled in his direction.

"What's up, Tony? You losing money?" He nodded at the *Wall
Street Journal* lying on Tony's desk. He grinned at him.

Micah came to a halt, shadowboxing in place. "Damn, Tony, you
know you ought to be ashamed of yourself fronting as a doorman.
You're almost the richest man in this city. Those old blue-chip stocks
of yours are gonna disintegrate before you decide to cash in."

Tony leaned back in his chair. He chuckled in satisfaction. "Shoot,
ain't any worse than you fronting as though you're going to the
Olympics. How many times are you gonna run in one morning?"

Micah quit shadowboxing. He pointed to Tony's coffee cup.
"What's in that cup? You sipping on the job again?"

Tony glanced at his cup. He bellowed out his gut-churning laugh.
"You save them there investigating skills for downtown. I know you
when I see you boy. You trying to see if I still got it, huh?"

Micah laughed too. "It's my job to make sure you're still up on the
game. I was just testing you, man. I'm making a lot of money off
those stock tips. So every once in a while I gotta make sure you still
got the eye and all. Just protecting my investment, man. Just protecting my investment. You can't blame a man for looking out for his
own." He shook his head at Tony. Then jogged out the front door.

Once he was on the street, Micah jogged as though demons were
chasing him. He flew by neighborhood stores and houses, running
to the park.

He sprinted out into the street. He played dodge with the oncoming
traffic. His limbs were so incredibly lithe, he glided through the morning rush.

When he reached the perimeter of Branch-Brook Park he picked
up his pace. He sped through his ten miles, pushing himself to the
limit. His sneakers smacked the blacktop of the runway like tiny tor-
pedoes being set off. Droplets of water gushed from his forehead.
Sweat lubricated his body as he ran on.

After his run, Micah walked slowly allowing his body temperature
to cool down. He went to the dry cleaners to pick up his clothes.

Sung-Yu greeted Micah as he walked through the door, fumbling in his pockets for his dry cleaning slip. "Morning again, Mr. Jordan-Wells," Sung-Yu said to Micah, "Did you forget something?"

Micah looked up from fumbling in his pockets, annoyed. A strange feeling shook him as he said "What the hell is wrong with all of you people this morning? I want my clothes. I forgot my slip."

Sung-Yu glanced at Micah as though he was losing it. Puzzled, Sung-Yu shook his head. "I'm sorry Mr. Jordan-Wells, I just gave you your clothes. You no remember? See." Sung-Yu plucked a dry cleaning slip from the stand on the counter.

Micah looked down at the slip. He turned around and raced out of the shop with Sung-Yu yelling after him, "I'm sorry, Mr. Jordan-Wells. I do something wrong?"

Micah ran down the street to his apartment building. He darted through the door running past Tony who looked up startled as Micah whizzed by him.

Micah ran to the stairwell in his building. He leaped up the cement steps a few at a time. When he reached his apartment he searched for an illegal entry. He saw none. Quietly, he inserted his key in the lock.

He entered the apartment cautiously. He pulled out his revolver and slinked against the wall. He peered around the corner going into his police stance. But no one was there.

Making his way to the kitchen, he saw the remainder of a breakfast he had never eaten on the table. Adrenaline pumped through his veins as he searched the rest of the apartment.

There was no one to be found. He went into the bedroom. Lying on the bed were his clothes from the dry cleaner.

Micah shook his head trying to clear it. He mentally retraced his steps for that morning. He never ate before he worked out. What the hell was going on?

A blinding pain seized him. He grabbed his head. Moaning he dropped to his knees. The pain in his head increased. He put his head between his legs to stop the terrible throbbing.

Micah fell into a deep abyss. The loud cries of agony emitting from the dead six-year-old boys pounded in his ears.

Their arms reached out to him in a silent plea. Their small faces were etched in fear. Slowly they backed away from him in terror. The silver glint of a sharp instrument shone in its metallic glory. "No! Please, no!" they whimpered. A creamy white substance foamed from their mouths.

The "X" branded on their foreheads connected him to his own eternity. It connected him to them. Micah looked down to see the mark of the "X" tattooed on the back of his right hand. It was faint but it was there.

The mime's face floated before him. He pulled a long, sad face at Micah. He knew the truth. Teardrops cascaded from his eyes. The mime's gestures loomed large in front of his eyes as he seesawed back and forth like a rag doll.

As he swayed back and forth, Micah could feel the jagged cut of throbbing, ripping flesh in his hands as he gashed at the skin. Then he gashed some more. He gashed until he saw the carving of a masterpiece.

The interpreter spoke. "Ronnie Schaefer says the man he saw commit the murder is Micah Jordan-Wells."

Micah couldn't stand this. He couldn't tolerate the things that happened when he was outside of himself. Through his blurred vision the room whirled around him.

He was in there. He saw it. The entire disgusting act. He'd done it before. He'd been there with the women. He peered through his eyes. Where was he now? All he could see was blackness. Everything was blocked. Why was he killing them? Why? Why? Why? It couldn't go on. He had to stop. Dear Jesus! Somehow it had to stop.

Insane laughter seeped through the walls of the room. The laughter surrounded him. It thumped through the Sheetrocked walls.

Micah lashed out, his arms thrashing wildly. Yet the laughter continued to swirl around him. It enveloped him in a blanket that was made for him. The "X" rose in its eminence. Grandstanding. Searing him. He felt the heat of it flow through his body.

It was a dance that had been orchestrated before his time. Written from the cradle to the grave. The handwriting was on the wall. All he had to do was find it.

Chapter 16

Derrick had made up his mind. He decided he would not be blown off by the likes of Shimmy.

Regardless of what it looked like or smelled like, he knew something was brewing. And it had a rotten feel to it.

Somehow, neither Silky's conviction nor his death had ended that feeling for him. He realized it had always been there but he had tried to push it off. Until Silky had burst into flames in court. That had set it off. He watched Shimmy purchase a cup of coffee from the corner coffee shop.

As Shimmy emerged from the shop, Derrick followed him. He tapped him on the shoulder from behind. "Shimmy, we really need to talk."

Shimmy whirled around spilling coffee all over his hands onto the ground. He glared at Derrick. "No we don't. I told you to leave it alone, Derrick. You don't want to mess with this. Drop it."

Shimmy turned to leave. He threw the remainder of his coffee in the trash leaving Derrick seething behind him. Derrick contemplated following him. But as he watched his rigid body movements he realized he wouldn't get what he needed from him.

It suddenly dawned on him that Shimmy was scared. That was very, very, unusual for the tough street historian. Armed with this new revelation Derrick decided he'd better dig deeper. He was going to step up the volume. What could possibly scare a man like Shimmy?

Later that night, Derrick was awakened from his sleep by a noise in the room. Sitting up in bed, he saw the wall of his bedroom burning. It was on fire. He jumped out of bed.

On a closer look, he realized that the fire was somehow contained. The flames were burning an image into the wall. Immobilized by shock, Derrick stared as an "X" seared itself into the wall.

He backed away from the flaming "X" tripping over some shoes on the floor. Air exploded from his chest. He banged his head on the bottom rail of the bed.

Rubbing the back of his head he looked up at the wall. The "X" extinguished then erased itself. The wall was clear of any image or hint of fire. Not even a smell of soot was in the air.

"No way!" He got up.

He went to the bathroom. He was trembling. He needed a drink of water. He had witnessed an evil so bold it had shown itself. Or did he? Was he dreaming? He pinched himself. He felt the pain. Hell no. He had seen it.

It had also given him his first real clue. The "X" was connected to Silky. It was the mark he had left on all the women he had killed. But Silky was dead. A shiver traveled along the back of Derrick's neck.

Derrick felt shaky but composed himself. This was a story that had the capacity to make his career. There must be a reason why he'd seen what he'd seen. Maybe some entity was trying to reach him. Wanted him to tell the story.

Hell, stranger things had been known to happen. He would record as well as report every detail. That was his job. He was a reporter. He wasn't going to be one of the corporate drones that only reported stories people could handle. No.

The truth wasn't always black and white. He knew that sometimes it lurked in the shadows. He just needed to connect the dots.

Chapter 17

Several days later cars were stacked and packed outside of St. Patrick's Cathedral where Rasheem Thompson's memorial services were being held.

Inside the church Micah stood rigid, dressed in black, looking like he'd just stepped out of the pages of the latest fashion magazine. He peered from behind his black shades at the crowd in the church.

The church was filled with uniformed and undercover police. It was not uncommon for a serial killer to show up at the services of one of his victims. Some of them liked to view the aftermath of their handiwork.

The television crews and print media were out in full force. They would record every teardrop that fell from Nakisha's eyes.

The press was watching Micah's next move. He was fresh off of Silky's case, which was still lingering in the public eye due to Silky's fantastic demise.

Before the ink was dry on the print from that episode, two children were dead. The murders had thrust Micah right back into the spotlight.

Micah had barely managed to keep certain details about the child murders out of reach of the media, such as Silky's trademark signature.

That information alone being released would have started a backlash of press. It would have created speculation that would have totally crippled his investigation as well as the Newark community. They could not afford to be mired in crackpots looking for their day in the sun by claiming responsibility for the murders.

Wolfgang had called in some serious markers to keep specific details of the murders from being released. Micah knew he had to move fast. Time was not on his side.

He turned his attention to Nakisha as she lit a candle and began to recite an emotional rendition of the Twenty-third Psalm. "The Lord is my Shepherd, I shall not want . . ."

Micah shifted restlessly as he silently eye-stalked the people who had crowded into St. Patrick's Cathedral. Suddenly, he realized Nakisha had finished her recital.

A soloist had stepped up to the microphone. She was delivering a hauntingly beautiful musical version of the song "Going Up Yonder." "If anybody asks you . . ." the lilting, spiritual notes rose from the singer's throat.

The melody and lyrics captured Micah. Something inside him crashed. He looked at the tiny pure white casket holding Rasheem Thompson.

A loud voice boomed in Micah's ear. "Dead boy walking. Dead boy walking." On top of the casket the dead boy tap-danced. He smiled at Micah. Then ripped open his burial clothes exposing his chest.

The "X" flashed blood-red, taunting Micah. He stretched out his arms. His head spun around once, a complete turn. Again he smiled.

Micah removed his sunglasses. He moved swiftly but with control through the mourners. Just as he reached the front of the church, the boy evaporated like mist into thin air. The soloist's voice soared.

The priest stepped to the front of the casket—which was undisturbed from what Micah could see. He sprinkled holy water over the casket. Several young men stood waiting. When the priest was finished they pulled the casket down the aisle of the church.

Micah stepped back. He put his shades back on to hide the wild look in his eyes. It was a good thing his movements had been smooth. Otherwise he would have interrupted the entire service with something he could not explain and that only he had seen.

Nakisha placed one foot forward, beginning her journey down the aisle, preparing to commit her son's body to the earth.

The priest held her arm, lending her support. The lyrics to "Going Up Yonder" cascaded like a waterfall around her as she followed the casket of her only child.

Pain and grief were etched into Nakisha's face as though her pain had been sealed in granite. The mourners stood in a silent salute as she passed by. Her sorrow was so tangible that even the media backed off respectfully. They conducted their work discreetly so as not to intrude on her very real suffering.

Quentin watched Nakisha's descent to bury her son. He also watched Micah Jordan-Wells.

Inside the tiny pure white coffin the slain boy lay in final peace.

Chapter 18

Micah's apartment was swarming with police officers. They crawled over every inch of space. The fingerprint experts were going to work.

Due to Ronnie Schaefer's ID of Micah as a murder suspect Wolfgang had to investigate. He had reluctantly ordered the search of Micah's apartment. Conspicuously absent was Nugent. He had decided against participating in the search of Micah's home so as not to have a hostile officer on the search, which might be prejudiced materially. Nugent was too close to Micah to be a part of the search, so he and Micah were at the precinct working on other aspects of the case.

Downtown, Micah stood in front of a map of Newark. Red pushpins marked the spots where the bodies of the little boys were found. Pictures of the deceased boys were scattered on the walls.

Nugent sprawled back in deep concentration with his feet propped up. He watched Micah pace in front of the map. Finally he said, "Any word yet?"

Micah stopped pacing. "Yeah. Some. There's no evidence of sexual contact with the boys and Silky's fingerprints were found at the scene of both murders." Micah dropped the last tidbit of information about Silky as though finding a dead man's fingerprints was a common everyday occurrence.

Nugent shot out of his seat like a cannon. His chair tipped over. "That's impossible."

Wolfgang walked in, interrupting their conversation. He sat at Micah's desk, sighing loudly. Tension emanated from every pore of the big man's body. "Micah, we searched every inch of your apartment. We did find some prints that are not yours."

Micah tensed. A look of hope streaked across his face.

Wolfgang waved it away. "The prints belong to Raven Oliver. The only other identifiable prints are yours."

Micah looked at him incredulously.

Wolfgang continued. "I know it's difficult to believe. But the only prints identifiable are yours and Miss Oliver's."

Micah's eyes turned to twin chips of slivered ice as he stared at Wolfgang, not believing his ears.

Rigidly, he spoke to Wolfgang as though he were speaking to a child who is hard of understanding, "I'm telling you, Wolfgang, the man had breakfast at my kitchen table. He was in my apartment. He picked up my clothes from the dry cleaners. He left them on my bed. Damn it!" Micah banged his hand on the desk.

He was beginning to lose it. The volume of his voice rose another notch. "There is no way he could do all of that without leaving a trace. What in the hell is going on here? He's not a ghost. He was there. So there must be some evidence of that. Send them back. They must have missed something."

Wolfgang got up to face Micah. "Micah, I talked to Tony. He loves you like a son. The man thinks the sun rises and sets with you. He said he saw you run early in the morning. He said he saw you run again later in the morning. He thinks you're secretly training for the Olympics. It's the same story with Sung-Yu at the dry cleaners."

Nugent braced himself for the oncoming onslaught from Micah. He didn't have to wait long. Micah stepped to Wolfgang until he stood nose-to-nose and eye-to-eye with him. He searched the depths of Wolfgang's eyes before saying in a tone dripping with antagonism, "It wasn't me."

"I know it wasn't." After a beat Wolfgang broke contact. He walked to the door of Micah's office. Micah and Nugent exchanged glances.

"Oh by the way, I'm releasing Ronnie Schaefer. I'm putting him in a place where he won't be found for a while. I can't afford any leaks and I can't leave him as bait for the press or anyone else's political aspirations. After all, this *is* Newark."

When he reached the door Wolfgang said, "One more thing. You might want to check on Silky's ashes. Seems he's leaving his fingerprints all over the place. It's a strange thing for a dead man to do. Don't you think?" He walked out the door closing it softly behind him.

Nugent pressed two fingers to the sides of his throbbing temples. "A ghost, you, and a dead man. I have a feeling this is going to get worse, a lot worse, before it gets better."

Chapter 19

The following morning six-year-old Byron Williams shuffled his feet playfully through the beautiful array of fallen autumn leaves. He looked up, loving all the colors he saw.

Byron was straggling quite a bit behind the other kids. He returned his attention to the electronic game he was playing. He was absorbed in the graphic characters that had come to life on the tiny screen he held in his hand.

Directly in front of him a man watched Byron, measuring his approach. Byron passed the tree where he stood. A hand reached out. He put a cloth over Byron's nose and mouth. Byron passed out without a whimper.

The delighted squeals and laughter of the other kids continued in the autumn air. They played games. They walked on to school, oblivious to the fact that another one of their own had been stricken.

Later that morning, Micah and Nugent walked the streets of downtown Newark. They tried to sort out the murders that were taking place.

The street was gearing up for the day's business. Vendors and street merchants were pushing their wares. A number of them waved in Micah and Nugent's direction. Shaughn Braswell saluted. They waved.

Micah was their very own celebrity. They considered him to be one of the coolest, smartest and slickest detectives Newark had ever seen. His smooth, suave manner was a continuous source of imitation.

Micah was completely unaffected by his own celebrity status. He knew he had a special entrée into the community. Keeping that entrée intact was more important to him than his celebrity status.

An old man dressed in heavy black winter clothing with a derby stuck on his head shuffled up to Micah and Nugent. He was a product of Newark's streets. One of the many relics left in the city.

Shuffling his feet, he looked directly at Micah and said, "God is good. God is great. God is good. God is great." He took his hat off and bowed in front of Micah—much to Micah's surprise. Then he shuffled on down the street.

The people of Newark were used to him. He did this all the time. These were the only words anyone had ever heard him speak. Although never before had he bowed to anyone.

What the people of Newark didn't know was that Isaac was a deeply spiritual man. In his inner coat pocket he carried the only two things he owned in the world: an old worn Bible that had been read so many times the pages were shorn and an old cross. It was made out of tree bark. It was identical to the one Micah wore. There were only four of them in the world.

Micah and Nugent walked in silence. Each of them pondered and weighed what they knew against what they didn't know.

Micah was the first to speak. "We've got to be dealing with a copycat, Nugent. He's using the same signature that Silky used on his victims."

"Yeah. Get that. The patterns are eerily the same too, man. Except that Silky killed women. These are little boys that are being murdered now. Why different victims? Why little boys all the same age?"

Micah spotted a break in the traffic on Broad Street. He nudged Nugent so they could run across the street.

"Well, the signature definitely connects the murders in some way. Maybe . . . maybe Silky was under orders all along. Maybe there's another killer we never knew about and Silky was the fall guy," Micah said as a brilliant moment of chilling insight seized him.

He would have liked to reject the idea. The thought of more than one like Silky was enough to freeze the blood in a person's veins. However, the idea refused to vanish or be vanquished. It parked itself firmly in the forefront of his mind.

Micah picked up his pace. He tried to figure out the pieces to the puzzle. It really didn't make sense. Nugent stayed steady beside him.

"Okay," Nugent said, "A serial killer's signature is like his calling card. It's how he does business. Right? How could the signatures be the same? Down to the stroking? How could the signatures be so exact and committed by two different people, Micah?"

Nugent grabbed Micah's arm. All of his pent-up questions poured out. "What's more how the hell do we explain Silky's fingerprints on the murders that are taking place now? The man is dead. We watched him burn. We watched him die. We saw it with our own eyes. This is getting really weird, man. I've seen murders and I've seen murders, Micah. But I swear if I didn't know any better I would think I'm losing my damn mind."

Micah was at a loss for words. He looked past Nugent. Gauging the weight of Nugent's words.

His head pounded. He bent over. He put his hands to his head. He righted himself after a short time. Micah shook his head to clear it as Byron Williams's voice exploded into his consciousness. "Mommy!" Byron wailed, "Mommy! Help me! No!" Byron began to cry.

Micah's face twisted. Agony streamed from his eyes. He concentrated. A sledgehammer blow slammed into his brain. Everything went black. He couldn't see. Then his vision cleared. When it did he looked at Nugent. Nugent watched him strangely. "What? What's up? What's the matter?"

Micah acted like he didn't know him. There was no recognition in his face.

Nugent didn't like this crap one bit. He scrutinized Micah. He didn't say a word.

Micah looked around. He didn't know where he was. He stared blankly at Nugent. His whole demeanor changed. His features, his appearance and his stance were transformed.

The new presence was commanding. Micah's entire being had altered in the blink of an eye. Before Nugent stood a man of monstrous, authoritative importance. He wielded great power. And he never slept.

Nugent was looking at a stranger inhabiting Micah's body.

Quentin Curry's voice rose up from the depths of Micah's throat. He assessed Nugent from behind Micah's eyes. He made his position abundantly clear. "When the seed of my enemy is removed all that will remain is for my seed to rule. The sixes and their carriers will be no more."

With that said, he released Micah's body leaving him on his own. Nugent didn't move a muscle. Recovering he said, "What the hell is wrong with you, Micah?"

For Micah there had been no lapse in time. He continued where he left off hearing Byron's voice. He looked at Nugent. "He's done it again, Nuggie. He's taken another kid."

Nugent tried to get a grip on the changing tide but Micah was not making this easy for him.

Micah took off in a dead run. Nugent was right behind him.

As they ran up to the police precinct, Derrick Holt spotted them. He called out Micah's name while running over to him.

Micah stopped. He turned around at the sound of his name. "Micah, I need to talk to you."

Micah shot him an exasperated look. "I said there will be no press on this case, Derrick. I know you got the message."

Derrick pressed forward, determined not to let the opportunity to speak to Micah slip through his fingers. "I want to talk about Silky. His story's not over. I know it and you know it."

Micah's eyes turned to glittering chips of crystal as he blew Derrick off. "Silky is dead. The case is dead. It's over, Derrick. Period. There is no story."

Derrick mulled this over, wondering why everyone kept trying to sell him on that.

He glanced briefly at Nugent, taking note of the little beads of sweat popping out on his forehead. Of course he'd been running, but still. "There's another story, one that didn't come out in court. I believe you know it."

Micah stepped to Derrick.

"And I believe your imagination is too active. Now get the hell out of here. Find some real work to do." Micah turned his back on Derrick. He ran up the stairs with Nugent right behind him.

Now wasn't that interesting? The cool, in-control Micah Jordan-Wells had a temper. The slick polish that he generally presented to the media was cracking. Derrick decided to push him all the way over.

"Micah! Satan is walking the municipal halls of Newark. He's leaving his mark all over the place."

Nugent tossed Derrick a strange look. A quiver inhabited his body at Derrick's words. Micah didn't even break pace.

When they arrived in the office, Micah searchingly looked around as though the right answers would suddenly appear before him.

Nugent asked, "What makes you think he's got another boy?" He searched Micah's eyes but found no explanation there.

"It's just a feeling."

There was a loud knock on the door.

Gaddy, the office reporter, gofer and sometimes comedian, stuck his head in the door. His usual gayness was missing. He wasn't smiling. He certainly didn't look like he was about to crack any jokes.

He glanced down at a report he was holding in his hand. "Micah, a report just came in. This isn't your area but we thought you might be interested because it involves a six-year-old boy."

The muscles in Micah's body tensed. Nugent shot Micah a questioning glance.

"Byron Williams never arrived at school this morning. The school notified his mother. She called in a missing person report on him."

"Where is his school?" Micah asked.

Gaddy glanced at the report again. "Ridgewood Elementary. Over in the area of Mt. Prospect Avenue." Micah's face went ashen.

Nugent looked strained. There was a decidedly peaked tinge to his coloring.

"Are any patrols out looking for the boy?" Micah said.

"As we speak. Maybe it's not tied in. From what we can gather the kid is a loner. The other kids saw him on the way to school this morning but he never arrived. Missing persons is combing the area and interviewing the mother. I'll keep you posted," Gaddy told him then closed the door.

After Gaddy left, Micah said to Nugent, "He's putting ass in my face. I live in that neighborhood. He's laughing at me, Nuggie."

Micah's phone rang. He snatched up the receiver. "Micah Jordan-Wells here."

A familiar laugh resounded in Micah's ear. Micah was startled. A voice from the dead floated over the wire.

Nugent watched as an electrified expression flashed across Micah's face.

Silky said, "Micah, I am risen. How do you like my new bag of tricks?"

Micah didn't answer. It was unmistakably Silky's voice. He didn't utter a word. He was stiff with disbelief.

"What's the matter? The cat got your tongue? Haven't you ever spoken to a dead man before? Well, here's something that'll loosen your tongue, my brother. Byron Williams is gonna die today unless you do what I say. It don't make me no never mind."

Micah swiftly recovered. He didn't know what he was dealing with but he would go to any lengths to save this kid's life and find out.

Adrenaline shot through his veins. He mouthed the word "Silky," to Nugent pointing to the phone. Nugent looked at him like he was crazy.

"Name it."

"Penn Station," Silky told him.

"Be there. Three p.m. is the hour. Wait by the shoeshine booth. Stand directly in front of the bank of phones. Don't bother trying to set it up because I'll know. I know all your moves, Micah. And by the way, I really enjoyed breakfast at your place. Except for your music. You've got some catching up to do, man." Silky laughed. The click of the phone sounded loudly in Micah's ear.

Micah looked at Nugent. "That was Silky. Three p.m., Penn Station is show time. Go get Wolfgang. Tell him Silky's been resurrected."

Nugent stalked angrily to the door.

He flung it open and turned back to look at Micah. "There is only one man in the history of the world that had the power to resurrect and his name ain't Silky." Nugent slammed the door behind him. He was tired of playing games with lunatics.

Chapter 20

That afternoon undercover police cased Newark's Penn Station. Micah Jordan-Wells strolled through the doors at precisely two fifty five p.m. as though he owned the place.

Penn Station was busy with out-of-town travelers as well as regular commuters running for trains, buses and taxis. People were checking schedules. Mothers were quieting down screaming toddlers and crying babies.

Micah strolled past the shoeshine booth. He nodded a greeting to the old shoeshine man, Bob. Bob was shining a customer's shoes. Upon seeing Micah, who was one of his favorite customers, he stopped and smiled.

Bob liked Micah. To him, Micah exuded class. Yet he was down-to-earth. Something Bob wasn't raised with in his time. He was also a great tipper and a Yankee fan to boot.

Bob loved the New York Yankees. He never missed a game. Whenever he shined Micah's shoes they traded opinions. Sometimes the exchanges got heated. When that happened they lasted through the whole shoeshine. It made Bob's day. He looked forward to Micah's shoeshine.

"Micah, can I get a shine for you today? I'll be right about done here in a minute."

Micah didn't break stride. He tossed an answer over his shoulder,

"Not today, Bob." He hesitated when he reached the bank of phones realizing he didn't know which phone to go to.

Scanning the bank of phones he spotted the phone that was for him. An "X" had been drawn on it in red marker. The haunting mark had insinuated itself into his life.

Micah looked at the "X" and it turned into a flame of fire. He took a step closer to the phone. The flaming "X" returned to simple red marker.

As he stuck his hand in his pocket the phone rang. He snatched it up. Silky's voice angrily sounded in his ear. "You brought a lot of flunkies, Micah. I told you not to do that. Get rid of them. Now! You've got five minutes." The phone went dead in Micah's ear.

Micah took out his walkie-talkie. Rapidly he spoke to Nugent. "He's on to it, Nugent. Get rid of every cop in the station."

"You can't do that. You won't have any cover. Wolfgang will—"

Micah cut Nugent off, flying into a rage. "Do it now! He's not playing ball! Lose them! Everybody, that includes you! You've got three minutes!"

Micah angrily clicked off the walkie-talkie. He watched the activity in Penn Station. He saw his orders being well orchestrated and carried out.

He took a deep breath. The phone rang again. He snatched it from the cradle. "It's your stage. They're gone. Now I want the boy. Alive."

Silky laughed, "Don't worry. You're going to get him. But he's hungry, so I need you to go to McDonald's."

Intense anger seared through Micah's body. "You like games don't you? Well, here's a game for you. There can only be one winner. Punk. You won't get away. I'm personally promising you that."

Silky laughed. It was a bone-chilling sound. His voice bristled at the sheer audacity of Micah.

Then, Silky's voice changed. The tone. The timbre. It was a voice Micah had not heard before. "I'll tell you what Micah. Just between friends. You can call me Criss Cross. Only my closest friends do that. You're a boy that pays attention. Close attention. You know my signature. Now. You know my name."

Micah was stunned. Before he could recuperate Silky's voice caressed his ear. "I told you your world as you knew it was no more Micah. I hate to keep repeating myself. Now you've caught me once.

But I've died and come back. I can do it again. I am the resurrected. Understand? I'm the man, Micah." Insane laughter rippled through the air.

The voice switched channels again. This time he spoke in the third person. "Criss Cross doesn't like to be crossed Micah, so why don't you be a good boy and go to McDonald's. Get the kid a Happy Meal."

There was another flip of the frequency. "Otherwise you're gonna make me blow. Then I'll deliver him to you piece by piece in candy wrappers. Come back to the phone when you're done."

Click.

He was gone.

"Great. That's just great," Micah, said, "A serial killer with the skills of a ventriloquist."

Micah's head was pounding again. He slammed down the phone. He knew Silky's voice when he heard it. Yet there was something else. Nothing in Micah's career had prepared him for this inside glimpse into hell.

One thing was crystal clear, he was playing in a different league. And this league had its own set of rules. Furiously he stomped his way over to McDonald's.

The restaurant was crowded. He was not in the position or frame of mind to wait at the end of a very long line.

Flashing his badge, Micah nudged his way rudely through the crowd. Seeing the badge people grumbled but moved out of his way. He reached the front of the line and stared at the clerk. The clerk gave Micah a baleful look.

"I need a Happy Meal," Micah told the clerk. The clerk, who was annoyed at Micah's actions, made a production of looking down and around Micah. Not seeing a child under twelve, he said, "Happy Meals are for children twelve and under."

Micah flashed his badge within an inch of the clerk's face. Exasperated, he was skidding just on the edge of his breaking point. Patience for the antics of this smart-mouthed punk was not in his program. "Just give me the Happy Meal."

The clerk shrugged and sighed. "Will this be for a boy or a girl?" Micah gritted his teeth and lost it. He'd had enough. He put a hand underneath his jacket feeling his shoulder holster. "Boy."

The clerk scurried to get the meal. He was sure he had heard the sound of metal clicking. This fool might shoot him over a Happy Meal. He handed it to Micah. Micah threw a twenty-dollar bill on the counter.

The Happy Meal in his hand he raced out of McDonald's without waiting for his change. On his way to the telephone he bumped into an old man who was dressed in rags. He neatly sidestepped the man. Passing him, Micah looked into his face and realized it was Nugent. Nugent winked at him. But Micah gave no sign of recognition.

When Micah reached the phone, it was already ringing. Quickly he picked it up. His heart thumped out a chaotic beat.

Micah had made up his mind as to what his play would be so he confidently said into the receiver, "I want to talk to the boy, Criss Cross." He'd had enough of the Silky game.

Criss Cross replied: "You're a quick study, Micah. I had you there for a moment though." He laughed. A long silence ensued.

Finally, Criss Cross said, "Well, now that Silky is no longer between us," he hesitated, "thanks to you he's gone. Poof. How about we play Go to the Head of the Class? You're a smart boy."

The hairs on Micah's skin crawled at the supreme arrogance emanating from the beast on the other end of the line.

Criss Cross continued, "If you don't piss me off maybe I'll give you a clue. Here we go. Weeeeeeeeeeeeeeeee." Byron's voice exploded in pure terror across the wire in Micah's ear.

"Mommy! I want my mommy!" The boy's voice was abruptly cut off.

Micah froze.

He looked around trying to get a handle on where their location might be. While he was searching, Criss Cross spoke, "What is the tie that binds, Micah?"

Micah hesitated a second too long.

"Sorry. Time's up. He's dead."

"No, wait! I know!" Micah yelled into the phone.

The boy's chilling scream sounded in Micah's ear. The loud report of a gun went off. Then there was a deadly silence.

"No. Oh, God. No." Micah dropped the phone. It dangled wildly in the air. The Happy Meal dropped to the floor. Micah raced through the station with his revolver drawn.

People scattered, running for their lives. Old shoeshine Bob backed into a corner. He ducked behind one of the shoeshine chairs. Never had he seen the twisted and chilled look that now formed Micah's features. Micah's eyes were shining like twin beacons of light in their sockets. Dark streams of it sprang from his eyes.

Micah had gone nuts. Penn Station erupted into pure fear and confusion. Nugent was now right behind Micah shouting at the crowds, "Everybody down. Get out of the way."

People scrambled and scurried trying to clear a path.

"He shot him, Nugent! He shot him while I was on the phone! Oh, God! Where the hell is he?" Micah looked wildly around but didn't see the target.

Quentin Curry watched the unfolding disaster from his vantage point. Then he disappeared.

Chapter 21

Inside the downtown branch of Newark's library, Derrick sat reading a headline from Silky's capture, "Micah Jordan-Wells Captures Newark's Notorious Serial Killer."

Derrick read the text, looking between the lines for subtle details. Maybe there was an angle he hadn't noticed before. The story had also been reported in the *New York Times*. He needed to see what their take was on it.

He looked around the library. He'd been really paranoid since the night of the flaming "X" in his bedroom.

He didn't see anyone so he continued reading, searching for the elusive. But he still felt someone or something was looking over his shoulder. He shook his head to clear the cobwebs.

While Derrick searched through old news clippings, Reverend Jackson was on a similar quest for information. He sat at his desk in his library.

Old time hymns floated softly from the radio while he absorbed the front-page picture of Micah in the *Star-Ledger* newspaper. He was obsessed over this picture. Something was there he couldn't quite put his finger on. It was disturbing. Carefully he studied the expression on Micah's face, searching for a clue.

A whooshing sound swept up behind him. He turned around to see the wall burning. The fire was contained. The wall itself was not actually burning. As he watched in fascinated awe, the flaming symbol of an "X" scrawled itself into the wall.

Reverend Jackson inhaled sharply. He moaned. A name escaped his lips. It was barely discernible. "Evelyn."

The reverend rose from his seat. He stared at the flaming "X" shaking his fist in rage at the absolute daring of the evil.

No longer able to contain himself, he said, "You are not the power. There is only one true power. Even though your deeds are dastardly, Quentin Curry, you are not the power! You're not it!"

The reverend walked closer to the wall. He screamed at the symbol of the "X." "Release Evelyn! I said release her. Now!" He watched, almost expecting Quentin to appear. He felt the heat of his glowing eyes although he could not see him. The "X" was the only sign he received.

Beads of sweat stood out on the reverend's forehead as he spent himself, trying to fight a darkness that was ready. The darkness was invading. The darkness was here. Its position was unmistakably clear. Darkness in its most sinister form had arrived.

The reverend trembled in fear. Rage crawled through his body. He reached for the telephone. It flew off the hook. It ripped right out of the wall. The telephone was flung across the room beyond his reach.

He whirled around just as the image of the "X" cleared itself from the wall. A look of swift determination settled on the reverend's face. He made the sign of the cross for the journey ahead.

Chapter 22

In the police lab, Wolfgang stared at Sidney Bowden, the charge officer on the Clinton Avenue murder.

Wolfgang couldn't believe what he had heard. "What do you mean Silky's fingerprints are missing? This is a secure area. There has never been a set of fingerprints missing in my entire career here."

Sidney shook his head at Wolfgang. "I know, sir. What can I tell you? Silky's fingerprints are missing." Wolfgang turned and walked out the door.

That night Micah and Nugent sat talking about the day's nightmare. "At least he revealed himself. We're no longer chasing a dead man or a ghost," Nugent said.

Secretly, Nugent was relieved at this bit of information. Both of these aspects were unsound to him, not to mention plain insane. It had been grating on his nerves big time.

"He hasn't revealed anything. We still don't know who he is. We just know who he's not. And we still don't know how the murders are linked."

Wolfgang walked in. "They found Byron Williams in the basement boiler room of Ridgewood Elementary School. He has the same M.O. as the other boys. Byron Williams was never shot."

Micah and Nugent traded a look. Micah's look turned deadly and undeniably wrathful. He broke his exchange with Nugent focusing on Wolfgang.

Wolfgang continued, "There was a voice recording found a few blocks from the school. A copy of a tape with the call Silky supposedly placed to you here, Micah. It has your prints all over it."

Wolfgang turned to leave the office under the heat of Micah's gaze without saying anything more.

A short time later, Nugent was on his way to the coffeemaker. It actually contained the world's worst coffee but Nugent desperately needed a caffeine jolt. Wolfgang stopped him before he had a chance to pour the awful black liquid. "I need to see you in my office, Nugent."

Once in the office, Wolfgang said, "Have a seat, Nugent."

Nugent sat down.

"Do you know where Micah was before the Penn Station incident today?"

Nugent shifted in his seat, "No. I was with him shortly before we arrived at the office. Then I met up with him at Penn Station, later."

Wolfgang entwined his fingers together. He studied them intently. Nugent knew this was a sure sign of stress.

"I've received a report that indicates a man who fits Micah's exact description was seen in the area where Byron was abducted early this morning. Micah lives in that area. The boy was dead long before the Penn Station disaster at three p.m."

Nugent leaned back in his chair. He didn't like the shift in the air. And he definitely didn't like where this was going. "Just what are you getting at, Wolfgang?"

Wolfgang sighed. "The tape with Silky's voice on it has a sophisticated remote electronic activation device."

Nugent slid to the edge of his chair. He ran a hand through his hair in total exasperation before banging his fist on Wolfgang's desk. "Oh come off it, Wolfgang! You're getting too paranoid here. Whoever placed that call is framing Micah. He knows that only Micah knows if he was really on the phone or not . . ." Nugent stopped in mid-sentence as he realized the powerful impact of his own words.

Wolfgang let the weight of Nugent's words hang in the air, before dropping his second bombshell.

"I've done a surveillance sweep of Micah's phone. There is no record of a call coming in. We picked up the ringing of the phone and that's it. There's no conversation, unless you count Micah speaking into the phone with no one talking back. Only Micah's voice is on the recording."

"The tape was found a few blocks away from the school. It looks like it was accidentally dropped in the killer's haste to get away. The recording was a replica of the conversation Micah claims he had with the resurrected Silky."

Nugent continued to glare at Wolfgang but said nothing.

"I also ran a voice sweep on the phone in Penn Station that Micah used. There was no conversation from the other end. In fact, there was no one on the other end. The only voice picked up on the line was Micah's. The surveillance was live during the conversation. I was able to tap into the line. Both times. The only voice on that line was Micah's. Period."

Wolfgang was now wringing his fingers together having graduated from simply entwining them. "I ran a check on Micah's cell phone line. The number to the phone in Penn Station showed up with the exact time it rang in Penn Station. Twice. It's beginning to look like the entire event was somehow staged."

Nugent couldn't think of what to say, so he decided he'd just as well say nothing. Nada. Not a word.

Micah stood outside of Wolfgang's office. He listened quietly to their conversation. When he'd heard enough, he stealthily crept away from the door.

Chapter 23

Evelyn sat in her parlor. The television was on. She was sketching an outline for her new historical romance in longhand.

The newscaster's voice broke into her thoughts. It pulled her attention away from the manuscript. She fastened her eyes on the broadcast.

"We interrupt this program to bring you a breaking story. A series of murders involving three six-year-old boys has gripped the City of Newark. From what we have learned at Eyewitness News the killings have all the signs of another serial killer on the loose."

Evelyn turned up the volume.

"There is some talk that the murders have the markings of ritualistic type killings. Newark's homicide department has not confirmed this information. The authorities are declining to comment at this time. We have learned that Newark's star homicide detective, Micah Jordan-Wells, has been exclusively assigned to the case. A police advisory is requesting that all children be escorted by an adult and not be left alone until the killer is found. We'll have more on these rising developments later."

Evelyn turned off the television. She took a sip from her cup of coffee. Going over to the liquor cabinet, she pulled out a bottle. She laced the coffee with Chivas Regal and took a long swallow. Draining the cup, she refilled it with Chivas.

She wandered over to the window, her hands trembling. Peeking through the heavy drapes, she saw Micah standing out front, staring at the house.

Puzzled, she waved, wondering why he was standing out front. But Micah didn't wave back.

Evelyn frowned. She took a closer look. Something in Micah's eyes made her blood run cold. She dropped the cup of Chivas. It spilled all over the Persian rug.

She hurried to the front door. Panic rose up from the depths of her belly as she realized she couldn't go out the door. "Damn!" she swore.

Still, she pressed on into the foyer. When she reached the front door she willed herself to at least open it.

Evelyn hyperventilated. Her breath was coming in wheezes, but she called out, "Micah!" as she looked across the lawn. The street was empty and deserted. Micah was gone.

Weeping Willow stared out the door behind Evelyn. Turning, she saw Quentin Curry as he was. He was the ultimate destruction of them all. In him was damnation. She covered her ears so she would not hear the shrieking. From beyond the realms, she would do what she must.

Later that night in Micah's office Micah and Nugent had files and papers strewn all over the place. They were both silent. They lived in the captivity of their thoughts.

Chapter 24

Micah had been up all night. His clothes were wrinkled. His shirt was open at the collar. His tie had been long ago abandoned. Light fuzz had sprung up along his cheek line. He looked like a rogue cop.

Soda cans, coffee cups and candy wrappers were strewn around the room. Milky Way wrappers were all over the place. It was Micah's favorite candy bar. He had polished off a bag of the miniatures during the night.

He rubbed a hand across the back of his neck, trying to rid himself of a cramp. He stretched out his long legs in front of him.

Looking over at Nugent he said, "No one at the jail ever reported Silky's fingertips were missing. They were shaved completely off. That must have been what the killer used at the murder scenes. Very clever. I'm sure Silky thought it was a great way to laugh at us from the grave."

"We should have known about that. I mean, damn, how many people are walking around without their fingertips? I can't believe someone didn't report it," Nugent said completely exasperated.

Micah grunted.

Nugent got up. He did a couple of knee bends. "It's a moot point now. Why did the killer use them?"

"He gets a kick out of being other people. He's a man of many faces," Micah said, "one of which appears to be mine."

Micah dug a little deeper. "He's playing us. He knew our first conclusion would be that there's a copycat killer. This dude isn't a copycat. He's an original. He was having fun with us with the Silky game. I'll be damned if he didn't pull off the voice. He knew we would have to investigate regardless of how it might look or smell. It's not like we're dealing with a rational mind here."

Nugent sat down. He decided to let Micah explain this out by himself. He listened as Micah spun his web.

"He's playing according to the rules of his own world, Nugent. A self-created imbecile." Micah stepped over the edge then fell into the pit of his anger. With extreme effort he dragged himself back into focus. Uncontrolled anger could get him killed.

Shrugging off the clawing feeling of lividness he said, "He calls himself Criss Cross. It fits with the sign of the 'X.' He likes to play head games."

Nugent watched Micah.

"He sounded just like Silky. The tape is a ploy. He's using the recording to try to frame me. Although, I haven't figured out how he got my prints on it. The bad thing is I think he's only begun to dig into his bag of tricks."

Nugent nodded.

Micah got up. He paced the room. "Alright. Let's tear this thing apart for the sake of argument. He used Silky's prints at the murder scenes. Say, the call he placed here was pre-recorded before Silky's death. That means they planned it. It means the two of them are connected."

Nugent rather reluctantly decided against telling Micah that a sweep of his phone showed no record of the conversation, except the actual ringing of the phone, which he himself also heard. Nor was he going to tell him there was no voiceprint of his conversation in Penn Station.

Nope. He didn't want to tell him that the only voice picked up in the sweeps had been his. Telling him could serve no purpose at this time. He continued to listen.

"Nugent we're dealing with a master serial killer. He's very secure in his own powers."

Nugent weighed Micah's words against the mounting evidence.

He tried to figure out how they could beat it before the pressure on Wolfgang was pushed to the limit. They were skating on very thin ice.

Micah stopped in front of the window. "Here's what we do know. He's a master planner. He's somehow connected to Silky. He's a power tripper to the nth degree. Power and control are everything to him. And the name Criss Cross coincides with the carrying of the 'X' that split open the middle of the boy's chest. The sign of the 'X' matches. So far he's demonstrating a vast amount of power."

"Yeah," Nugent said, "well right now he's holding all the power until we find the connection."

Micah was quiet. A thought niggled at him. It was just at the base of his consciousness. Something they missed.

Micah started rifling through files. He found the one he was looking for. He opened it spilling out the contents.

Nugent came over as pages of obituaries of the dead women scattered across the desk. Their faces smiled hauntingly at them.

Micah scanned the contents. Suddenly a piece of text literally jumped off the page at him. Six-year-old son. Six-year-old son. Six-year-old son.

Micah's heart raced. "That's it!"

"What's it?"

Words tumbled out of Micah's mouth with the speed of light. "All of the women Silky murdered had one thing in common. I mean outside of beauty, youth, and the fact that they all lived in Newark."

"What's that?"

"They were all the mothers of six-year-old sons. Look at this." He passed the information to Nugent.

"Every single one of them, Nuggie. Every one of them had a six-year-old son. I think they were selected for that reason. What are the odds that all of those women would just happen to have six-year-old sons?"

Micah paced the room. Nugent felt that common thread that ran through both of their veins at the same time whenever they hit on something important in a case. "I'm feeling you," he said.

"It's a hell of a coincidence. And, it links them. Damn it! It links them in a way we never thought of before. Maybe Silky's mother didn't want him. Maybe she gave him away when he was six," Micah said.

Nugent ran with the ball. "A psychological link. He was killing his mother." The tentacles of Nugent's thoughts reached out to entwine with Micah's. Now they were vibing.

"Exactly," Micah said. "Frequently, in case after case, we've seen that serial killers often have some childhood trauma that relates to the type of murders they commit. Not in all cases, but in enough of them to make it a viable point."

"That's true," Nugent replied as he absorbed the information that was now processing through his brain at the speed of a nanosecond.

"Okay," Micah said, "the tie that binds. That question has been left at every one of the boys' murder scenes. Criss Cross asked me the same question. When I didn't answer quickly enough the child screamed. A shot was fired. The answer is a child to his mother. It's the most binding tie in life. She rejected him—the murdered women. She didn't want him—the murdered boys. Full circle. One and then the other. Silky, then the illusive Criss Cross."

Nugent exhaled.

"Both of them are probably rejects," Micah stated with satisfaction.

For the first time Nugent heard something that made sense. A dawning horror seized him with the blow of a sledgehammer. He sucked in a deep breath. "Oh my God! There are two of them. They committed the murders in stages. Silky was only the beginning."

Micah smiled. "Dead on. Silky was only a piece of the puzzle. One damned piece."

Micah ran down Criss Cross's mental profile. "He's inferior. Insecure. He's twisted. Killing the boys is a punishment. The man is in a rage, Nugent. He's ripping them up. Marking them."

"Yep. He's extinguishing them."

"Because murdering them is not enough," Micah said. "He's pushing them into nonexistence. That's why he brands them, scribbling his signature on their carcasses. He's a sick bastard."

"The sixes and their carriers will be no more," Nugent said, the deadly threat springing from his lips.

Micah looked at Nugent sharply, "What?"

Assessing Micah's reaction, Nugent shook his head. "I'm sorry. I was just spacing, man. Anyway I have two questions. Why didn't Silky kill the six-year-old boys of the mothers he murdered? And why would the murders of different boys start after his death? He could have killed the six-year-old boys that belonged to the mothers."

Pictures of the surveillance tapes taken of Silky flashed through Micah's mind. Knowledge opened like a rose. "Silky was a cold-blooded psychopathic murderer with one human flaw."

"What was that?"

"I'll show you." Micah retrieved the surveillance videotape from the file cabinet. He popped it into the VCR. Nugent sat on the edge of the desk. A series of images appeared on the screen.

Silky stood behind a fence in the park watching the little leaguers play softball. In another image he shot hoops with some young kids in the playground. The next image captured him buying a kid an ice-cream cone. The look on Silky's face in each of the clips was one of parental concern.

These images revealed a side of Silky completely at odds with his role as Newark's worst murderer. The portrait was tinged. It was slightly off balance.

Silky knelt down in front of the kid with the dripping cold treat. He gently wiped the ice cream from the corner of his mouth.

Micah froze the frame. Nugent gasped as the walls came tumbling down.

"Criss Cross has got to do the kids himself. Silky worshipped kids. Probably thought he was doing the kids a favor getting rid of their no-good mothers. Killing kids went against his grain. I'll bet this was the one area where he couldn't be controlled. Because somehow Criss Cross *was* controlling him."

Nugent exhaled for the second time in their exchange.

Micah was excited. He was on to it. He felt it in his bones. Nugent felt it, too. They didn't have all the pieces. But, like joggers who run a well-known track, they knew they had hit their groove.

"Nugent, we have to look for six-year-old boys who were given away. Let's start with foster care. Check the adoption agencies. Maybe that's what they have in common. Silky hates the mothers. Criss Cross hates the kids and the mothers. Silky was a follower. Not a leader."

Micah ejected the tape.

"Silky was under orders all along. It makes sense now. Remember how we said it seemed almost as though he was an observer at the murder scenes. As though he was looking through someone else's eyes. His murders were like portraits."

Nugent nodded, remembering.

"Somehow Criss Cross was using him like a conduit. I don't know, maybe through some kind of a ritual. Criss Cross was present at the murder scenes of the women at some level. I'm sure of it. When Silky's time was up, Criss Cross was ready to come out of the closet. And now he's out in full force."

Nugent shook his head. "At some level? Either he was there or he wasn't."

A lightning flash laid hands on Micah, tossing him into Silky's body at the scene of the crime. He could see it all. *Oh my God!*

As though nothing had happened, Micah said, "It's not that simple, Nugent. Something out of the ordinary is going on here. At the sentencing Silky said that I had captured him. But, I hadn't captured all that there was. He said my world, as I knew it, would be no more. He talked about smoke and mirrors. And, we are definitely playing smoke and mirrors here. Hide and seek. Don't you think?"

Nugent nodded.

"All right then. The only way we're going to catch him is not to rule anything out. We've got to think outside the box. No matter how incredible it might seem. Otherwise we're gonna be seriously played."

Again, Nugent nodded. He knew that Micah's capture of killers was legendary. He'd learned a lot from him in his time. Micah had not gotten where he was by thinking like those around him.

In the past Micah had come up with some far-reaching theories. Those very theories were what allowed him to catch the killers. Not one of those theories had ever been listed in the police manual. And not one of them had gone by the book.

Besides, if he and Micah didn't come up with something viable soon, there was a good chance Micah himself could be charged with the murders.

There was no doubt things were getting shaky on the outside. Wolfgang was stretching himself to the limit keeping things under wrap. But the clock was ticking. They were dancing on a tightrope.

Anyway, he didn't believe Micah was the murderer. He knew he wasn't. Regardless of how it looked. But he'd be the first to say that it looked real bad.

"Okay," Nugent said. "Is Criss Cross randomly choosing six-year-old boys?"

"He's leading us. He knew that once Silky was dead and these murders began, eventually we would make the connection. I'm not sure if they're random or specifically selected. But we'll find out. What matters to him most is: one, that he kills and leaves his mark and, two, that he taunts in the process. He's flaunting what he thinks of as his superiority."

Micah sat down behind his desk. "Which brings me to another problem. If we're on the right track with this, then Derrick Holt from the *Star-Ledger* is a thorn in our side, because he's acting like a dog in heat when it comes to Silky."

"I think we may have found the link to catching this maniac, but that means nobody can get to that information before we do, Nugent."

"I'm on it," Nugent said.

Nugent hesitated then issued Micah a warning. "Be careful. What if he wants you to find him, on his terms? You're walking in Criss Cross's mind. Or maybe he's walking in yours. Either way it's a dangerous walk."

Their eyes locked.

A silent understanding passed between them. "I know. I can feel him. But it's the only way I can catch him."

Chapter 25

Derrick sat in City Hall at a dusty old table poring over old birth records. He wiped the tiredness from his eyes with the back of his hand.

He had been squinting in dust for quite a while. He decided to make some photocopies of the documents he'd found to take with him. Then he'd call it quits for the night.

When he arrived outside he found that all of the tires on his car were flat. A red "X" was painted on the windshield of his car.

He looked up and down the street in frustration. He kicked the wheels of his car in a rage. He was getting tired of this now-you-see-me, now-you-don't crap.

Out on the New York harbor Shaughn Braswell and Quentin Curry stood side by side on the pier looking out over the water. The sky was clear as several boats cruised by on liquid waves.

The island of Manhattan seemed blanketed in tranquility. Shaughn was in a rare and reflective mood. He watched the captain of one of the boats steer it smoothly through the waters. The floating ripples the boat left in its wake mesmerized him.

Shaughn said to Quentin, "You know, in a different time and in a different place, I might have done that."

Quentin turned the full force of his magnetic gaze on Shaughn. "What is it that you might have done, Shaughn?"

Shaughn smiled, revealing charm along with his drop-dead good looks. He looked like a young man just out enjoying the evening. He pulled the collar of his parka closer around his neck as a cool breeze blew in from the water.

His long ponytail swayed in the wind. "Sail boats," he told Quentin. "I'd like to feel the power of the steering wheel ripping through the waters. Be in command of the waters. I like the freedom it represents." Almost nostalgically, Shaughn said, "I'd like to feel free. Just once."

Quentin turned to Shaughn with a demonic intensity that bristled through the air. He raised his arms creating a storm of immense proportions. The storm blew like a raging wind over the harbor.

The boats on the water rocked and swayed. The wind howled and shrieked, blowing away everything in its path. Trash cans overturned. A fanatical dust storm rose in their midst. With one sweep of his hand Quentin had turned a tranquil scene into a nightmare of blazing levels.

Quentin didn't blink an eye. His pupils turned fiery amid the turmoil. The fiery pupils locked on Shaughn. Flames of fire sprung from their depths. "There is no other time. And there is no other place, Shaughn. Do not dishonor me by wishing for the trivial things of the common man. I am power."

Lightning flashed. The wind blew more fiercely. Quentin and Shaughn stood in the midst of the storm in one of the oldest face-offs on earth.

"Your mission in Newark is simple, Shaughn. The carriers of the sixes and the seeds lounging in their loins must be eliminated. They are my enemy. The merging of the power must take place. It will take place."

Quentin pointed to the sky. His rage was palpable. "He is trying to make a fool of me. Look." Quentin held out his hand. A vision unfolded.

He showed Shaughn the backs of the heads of the three murdered boys. At the right base of the hairline, very faintly etched just above the neck area, practically invisible to the normal eye, was the number six. A wave of Quentin's hand and the vision was gone. Shaughn stared at him.

Quentin took a cigarette from his jacket pocket. He lit it. Slowly he pulled the smoke into his lungs.

"The people who carry that mark can upset the balance of power. My power. There are only a chosen few of them. We are doing well in the elimination of them, so far."

Quentin took another pull on the cigarette. He turned to look out over the stormy waters. Shaughn watched him but didn't speak.

"There is still work to be done, Shaughn. That is your job. He tried to trick me because the boys of the women didn't carry the mark. Only the women were carriers. The boys who were just murdered would have grown up to implant the seeds, which would produce warriors at the ready, when the war on earth comes. Newark is the chosen ground."

Shaughn nodded. "All of them will die." His voice carried out over the howling winds. It floated across the waters.

Quentin smiled. Then he turned to the waters. A wave of his hand and the storm receded.

Shaughn had found his way back into Quentin's good graces, and he listened. "Do not underestimate Micah Jordan-Wells. He is a major stumbling block. As such he must be destroyed."

Chapter 26

It was time to perfect his masterpiece. Shaughn sat at his work-table. He worked steadily on the sculptured bust. He scrunched his eyes in concentration.

His fingers kneaded the final touches to the clay. They moved with deftness. They possessed the sureness of a true craftsman. His head was bent over the bust attending to the final details. When he finished he leaned back to admire his sculpting.

A smile touched the corner of his lips. He daydreamed into the serenity of Raven Oliver's eyes.

Shaughn picked up his cell phone. He punched in some digits.

"Hello. Raven's Boutique. How may I help you?" Raven's lilting tone floated sensually over the wire.

"Raven. How's my baby today?" Shaughn said in the perfect imitation of Micah's voice.

Raven smiled. "Micah. I've been worried about you."

"Maybe I can ease those worries tonight. How about dinner at seven? At Maroon's on 16th in the city?"

"I'll see you there. Don't you dare be late."

"I won't," Shaughn said intimately. He clicked off. He leaned down to the face of the bust. He kissed each eyelid softly.

*   *   *

Raven cradled the phone. A warm smile played across her face.

Brandi stopped going through the racks of dresses. She cut her eyes at Raven. She didn't even need to ask. She knew by the expression on Raven's face that Micah had been on the phone. "On again, huh?"

Raven looked at her. "You don't like Micah, do you?"

Brandi replied truthfully, "I want to see you have some fun. Micah never has time for that. And yeah, there is something. He just doesn't totally add up in some way, Raven. There's something about him."

Raven didn't have a problem with Brandi speaking her mind. Brandi was bold. She always had been. She could deal with what Brandi considered her truth. She decided to sprinkle a little of her own truth on top of Brandi's. "Brandi, there is something about Micah. He's charismatic, mysterious and fly, girl! Every time I peel away a layer," her voice took on a dreamy quality, "I find something else. Micah is definitely worth waiting for."

Brandi turned back to the racks of dresses. She rolled her eyes. She could spot game a mile away. She snorted. "Humph. He'd better be. I got my doubts about your chances for a real life with him, though. And I just hope you don't find a surprise under one of those layers. Go ahead. Peel away."

Raven decided to put some distance between her and Brandi's pessimistic attitude. She refused to allow her to spoil her day. "I'm going over to the women's shelter. I want to spend some time with Maya and her son before I get ready for my date with Micah."

"Suit yourself," Brandi said. Normally she wouldn't have been so short with Raven. She knew Raven's work at the battered women's shelter was important to her. She loved the time she spent with those women and their kids.

Raven frequently donated her time. She also donated clothes from the boutique. She had helped many of the women get on their feet, find employment and places to live.

She bought toys for those kids in abundance. She also made cash donations to keep the shelter running. But sometimes Raven wracked her last nerve because she was blind as a bat when it came to Micah Jordan-Wells.

Raven ignored Brandi's edginess. Her mind was filtering through outfits of what she would be wearing for dinner with Micah. Brandi's reply was already trailing in the winds of the past.

Shaughn stood admiring himself in the mirror. He was buff, lean and smooth. He loved it. He turned away. When he turned back a different reflection peered back at him. His demeanor, posture, and stance had changed.

Vaughn was six years old. He was Shaughn's alter personality. He struggled to push his way out to the forefront. There was a slight pop, like electricity, and Vaughn was out visiting.

Vaughn said to Shaughn, "You have a date with a lady." He giggled. "Is she pretty?"

The body demeanor and posture changed again. Shaughn's tone was supremely arrogant. "Yeah. She is. She belongs to Micah. And tonight, I'll get to sample Raven. I'll get to devour all that he cherishes."

There was another quick popping sound. Vaughn struggled to make his way to the forefront once again. "I don't want to sample Raven. I want my mommy. Can I see her, Shaughn? Please?"

Shaughn pushed Vaughn out of his place. When he was back his eyes flashed fire. "Stop being a baby. You'll see her when I say you can. You'll see her for sure when you return to hell because that's where she'll be. That's where we'll all be." Shaughn's eyes took on a faraway look. "Down in the bowels of the earth," he laughed.

Vaughn started to cry. He and Shaughn struggled for first position in the body. Shaughn and then Vaughn. Vaughn and then Shaughn. Shaughn's body took on the characteristics of a floppy rag doll. They twisted and winded, back and forth. They fought each other fiercely for the dominant position.

Shaughn was a great deal stronger than Vaughn most of the time. But when Vaughn really wanted something, he cried and he fought.

Vaughn pushed with all his might. He pushed with a vengeance. Shaughn toppled out of the dominant position. Once Vaughn regained control he pushed Shaughn down into the deep. The deep was the inner place where the personality resided who was not in the dominant position.

Satisfied Vaughn sat down on the floor cross-legged. He pouted his lips as tears streamed from his eyes. He told Shaughn, "Mommy. I want to go see my mommy."

Shaughn was tired. He most definitely was not in the mood for Vaughn's whining. Sometimes he'd stay in the deep and let Vaughn stay out and play, just to pacify him so he didn't get in the way later on.

Unfortunately, Vaughn had now pissed him off. He wanted time to get ready for his date with Raven. So with one Herculean yank he snatched Vaughn down into the deep. Taking the body back, regaining full control of it. Vaughn gave a startled whimper as he plunged down into the dark place.

Shaughn stood up. He looked in the mirror. He walked over to the bust of Raven to kiss each eyelid again. He could taste this girl. He couldn't wait. She was fine with a capital F. And she was Micah's.

Vaughn was in the deep dark place now. Shaughn had an iron grip on him. He couldn't move. He could hardly breathe. He retreated, letting Shaughn have the body for now. He hadn't even gotten to color in his books while he was out, or ask for raspberry sherbet.

That night, Shaughn Braswell sat across the table from Raven. He was an exact replica of Micah Jordan-Wells. He possessed the clean-cut look, the voice, the tone, and the very mannerisms of Micah.

Raven glowed. Excitement flowed through her body. At last she was having a private dinner and some time with Micah. Her excitement was contagious.

Shaughn smiled at her excitement. He looked at her captivatingly across the dinner table.

He leaned over and smoothed back a lock of Raven's hair, placing it gently behind her ear. It was the same gesture Micah always used with her.

He looked deeply in her eyes. He touched her on the cheek. It was a feathery stroke pent up with conveyed longing. The physical wave of it reached out to touch her, "Let's get out of here."

Raven looked at him tenderly. "I love you, Micah."

Shaughn leaned across the table. He flipped his tongue in her mouth, sucking her into a sexual cyclone. Fever lit her throat. Fire ignited her body. Only Micah could do that. His longing tasted salty on her lips.

"I know you love me," Shaughn told her.

Chapter 27

In her Victorian parlor, Evelyn sipped from a cup of coffee. She sat straight, her body rigid. Across from her, the persistent old reverend gazed in her direction.

Reverend Erwin Jackson had just come from The New Jersey Institute of Living—the orphanage where he spent a good deal of his time. He was running the entire ministry now. On the long drive to Evelyn's he had suffered in the spirit at the thought of his pending confrontation with her.

Evelyn had listened to all her favorites this morning, Beethoven Symphony #9 and Liszt. The music had now stopped. Actually, if she were honest with herself, the music had really stopped long ago.

It was increasingly difficult for her to become lost in the soaring genius notes that poured out of the recordings. To let her mind fly as though it possessed wings of its own. She sighed deeply at the loss.

Evelyn took another sip before she began what she thought of as her monologue with the reverend. Something dark, and deep, floated from her eyes to peer across at him.

A sense of great sorrow seeped from her pores. "Why don't you just let it go, Reverend? It's bigger than both of us. There's nothing I can do. I have no proof. She hesitated, "Even if I did . . ." Her voice trailed off into nothingness.

The reverend leaned forward in his seat. It was urgent that he get through to her. He knew Evelyn had built a wall around herself; one even he was having trouble penetrating. Nevertheless, there was too much at stake. He must get through to her, no matter what it took.

"You have two powerful weapons, Evelyn. You have the truth. And you have your faith. If you don't use them, you're going to lose the most precious thing in your life."

The reverend rose from his chair. He knelt in front of Evelyn.

"If you do not come forward soon . . ." he searched the depths of those twin dark pools that were beholding him. "If you don't, then I will be forced into a difficult position. This is a war of the spirit. It must be fought as such."

The reverend stood up. He slid the seat a little closer to her so he could be in more direct eye contact. He took his seat again. "I am not as frightened as I once was. I will use what I know." His tone left no doubt as to his conviction.

Evelyn sat forward in her chair, leaning toward him. Her empty coffee cup tumbled from her hands. She didn't pick it up. Her eyes flashed a fire that hadn't been present in her in a long time. "Don't be a fool, Reverend. Quentin will destroy you. Let it be. You don't know for sure."

The reverend gazed around the parlor. It seemed even darker than usual. The room had a very somber feel to it.

He shook off the cloying feeling of the room's spirit. He spoke to Evelyn in evenly clipped tones, "I know this. Micah Jordan-Wells will be destroyed unless you or I tell him the truth. He's your son. For God's sake, Evelyn."

Evelyn shivered. The screeching reached her ears. She refused to grasp the implications. As the reverend watched, Evelyn retreated. She was no longer able to deal with this, so she simply blanked the reverend out.

The reverend watched her. Then he said, "Evelyn, you must save your son." He realized his statement had fallen on deaf ears. He pushed back his chair. He squinted. He could have sworn he had seen a shadow. Something had flitted across the foyer. He looked closer. There was nothing. He shrugged.

The reverend came to a silent decision. He prayed for the strength he knew would be necessary to carry him across a sea of great evil.

He knew the principalities of darkness were descended right there in their lives. It was alive and in full effect. He prayed for faith. He prayed for the strength. He also prayed from the depths of his being for the life and soul of Micah Jordan-Wells.

He knew that the biggest problem with evil was that most people didn't really believe it existed. It did. The reverend let himself out.

A short time after he left, Evelyn rose. She picked up her cup off the floor. In the kitchen, she poured a fresh cup of coffee.

Lethargically, she returned to the parlor. Upon entering the parlor, a scream of magnified proportions flew from her mouth. It soared through the room, gaining in momentum, gaining in pitch.

Every piece of furniture in the parlor had been moved. All of it had been rearranged. She could hear the music from the past. The melody of it assaulted her ears, spinning her back in time. There had been a gala party. Beautifully dressed people. Gay, happy, they were laughing. The parlor hadn't looked like this since Evelyn was a very young child.

But there was more than that. A huge mural dominated the center wall. There was a vivid depiction of two people. It was alive, in motion. It was vibrant with movement, slithering, humping movement. The colors were stark.

The bodies of a man and a woman writhed in harmony. Their bodies bucked tightly together. The woman's head was thrown back, in the throes of ecstasy. Her mouth was wide open; her eyes were glazed with the type of intimacy that would be considered a cardinal sin.

Behind them was an exact replica of the parlor as it had been then. It had happened in this room. Evelyn looked down. One of the man's feet was hanging from the sofa. The screams stuck in her throat. Evelyn gagged. Then she fainted.

Weeping Willow leaned over in her ear. "Evelyn, the reverend is right. You must save your son."

A splash of cold water hit Evelyn's face. She woke up sputtering. She looked around. The parlor was exactly as she had left it. There was no depiction on the wall.

She must have been dreaming again. She couldn't stand to dream.

Weeping Willow floated up the staircase to her room. Her face was drenched in tears. It was no use. Evelyn would be no help at all. She was held too firmly in his grip.

Another way would have to be found. That way would have to be Micah Jordan-Wells.

Chapter 28

Micah and Nugent sat with parts of Silky's file spread out between them. Each of them lost in their own thoughts.

Nugent broke the silence. He looked at Micah, seeing the wear and tear the case was taking on him. "Micah, you should take a break from staying all night. You're killing yourself, man."

Micah just grunted in his direction. He looked at Nugent, not seeing him. His mind was in a faraway place. He fingered the papers from the file in his hand. Then he said, "The criminal psychology section is missing from this file. I'm going to pay Patrick Hayes a visit. I'd like to go over the evaluation on Silky."

A soft knock sounded on the door, interrupting them. Nugent said, "Enter," in a preoccupied tone.

Raven, a striking-looking figure in crimson red, swept into the office.

Both Nugent and Micah stared at the vision she presented. She floated into the room. Her vibrant warmth, the regal bearing she possessed, overshadowed the gloom that had settled in the room.

A smile lit up Micah's face at the sight of her. It had been too long since he'd spent any real time with her. He missed her. The sight of her slammed home this fact. Warm liquid flowed through his body.

Raven tossed out a greeting to Nugent as she headed for Micah.

"Nuggie," she used the nickname that Micah had for him, "You're still looking as good as ever."

Nugent blushed. He lowered his eyes as he shook his head. "You're a lethal weapon that Micah should keep under lock and key."

Raven laughed. "Well, he did a pretty good job last night. But he lets me out to play during the day." Her casual remark dropped like a rock in the midst of the room. The smile faded from Nugent's face. Micah looked at Raven as though she'd lost her mind.

Raven felt the sudden shift in temperature in the room. She stopped in her tracks. She looked from Micah to Nugent. "What? What? Why are you staring at me? Did I grow two heads? What?"

Micah stalked over to stand in front of Raven. His eyes were two penetrating beams of light. "What do you mean about last night?"

Raven reached out a hand to touch Micah's cheek. He caught her wrist in midair in a viselike grip.

Startled at his reaction, Raven said, "Micah, let go of me. You're hurting me."

Nugent quickly covered the distance to where Micah and Raven were standing. His brain shouted out a denial as the realization of what must have happened swept his consciousness.

Nugent looked at Micah. He silently pleaded with his eyes, as Micah held Raven's wrist in his grip. Micah didn't blink an eye. A cold frozen glance, dipped in black hatred, wrapped Nugent in its tentacles.

The air in the room took on the same frigid iciness that was reflected in Micah's eyes. Micah's stance had changed to that of a madman. The madness was on the verge of leaking out everywhere.

Nugent didn't want to make the wrong move by touching Micah. He thought quickly. "Micah, she doesn't know."

Micah released Raven. She rubbed the area where he had gripped her. A red angry welt was popping out on her wrist. The print of his fingers was embedded in her skin.

Micah's eyes flashed white-hot anger. Hatred spilled out from behind his pupils at Raven. It boiled up from the pit of his stomach, splashing all over her. She took a step back as though she'd been struck. Hysteria held her as her windpipe closed, stricken with the pain of unshed tears.

Raven managed to croak out the words from her constricted windpipe, "What? What is it I don't know? What is going on?"

Micah took a last look at her. "Get out. Just get out."

Incredulous disbelief flashed across Raven's face. Through no will of her own, she screamed, "Micah!"

Nugent knew when enough was enough. This was definitely enough. He took Raven's hand. He propelled her through the door of the office before she could protest.

Raven struggled against Nugent. "No! Wait! What's wrong?" Finally she started to cry. She just couldn't help it. This was too much. "Nugent, what's wrong with him?"

Nugent closed the door to the office. "Come with me." He headed to Wolfgang's office with Raven in tow.

Micah stared out the window. The door to the office slammed. He heard the sound of Raven's hysterics on the other side of the door. Her hysterics grew fainter and fainter. Nugent was leading her away from the office. A stream of light streamed from Micah's eyes connecting with the desk.

Micah stared at a paperweight on the desk. It exploded into a ball of fire. He focused on different objects. At his glance the objects exploded.

He stepped back to look at the disaster he had created. The utter realization of what he'd done dawned on him. He put his hands to his head.

A severe headache seized him in a vise-like lock. He took another step back trying to distance himself from his own destruction. He tried to step back from his own malice.

He was tossed back into the courtroom. In front of him a vivid scene from the past was taking place. He saw Silky burst into flames.

Criss Cross's voice exploded in his head. "Whoosh. Thanks to you, he's gone. Poof."

A moan escaped his parched lips, "No. No."

Micah went to the men's room. He walked over to the mirror. He looked at himself. A desperate look of denial stared back at him. His eyes were illuminated. His cheekbones were chiseled in granite. Hard. Smooth, like a person locked in death.

Micah couldn't take his eyes away. The mirror melted under the sheer intensity of his gaze. A heat rose up from his eyes. His image melted away in the molten glass. Beyond the melted glass embedded in the wall his image remained, intact.

His reflection stared back at him. Micah grabbed his head. He moaned again, "No."

He hit the wall with such force it rocked him backward. He fell on the floor. He rolled around like an animal in the throes of pain. Bile streamed up from the pit of his stomach. It spilled out of his mouth.

On the cold, hard tile floor, on his knees, he looked up at the wall to find his image still imprinted into the wall. It continued to stare at him.

Raven dabbed at her red-rimmed eyes with a tissue. She looked from Wolfgang to Nugent as though they had totally lost it. Unable to hold back her feelings, even for Micah's boss, she said, "You're crazy. You're all crazy. I don't believe a word of this madness."

Nugent squatted in front of her. "Raven, Micah didn't leave his office all night last night."

Raven blew her nose. She geared up for the confrontation with Nugent. She wiped her nose. Then she put it within an inch of Nugent's face.

She enunciated every word, "What . . . are . . . you . . . talking . . . about? Micah was in my bed last night. He made love to me. I've been with Micah for five years. I know every inch of him. Damn! What are you? Some kind of lunatic?"

Nugent exchanged a quick glance with Wolfgang. Then he looked into Raven's eyes. Finally, he bowed his head.

Wolfgang watched Raven. He saw what he believed might be the first ray of hope. He wasn't totally sure. But his gut told him that this girl might have the answer he needed.

Wolfgang was descended from a long line of policemen. His great grandfather had been a cop. So had his grandfather, his father and an uncle. Instinct was built into his genes.

Wolfgang went over to Raven. His voice held absolute authority. His tone brooked no argument. "Raven, I have to place you in protective custody immediately. I'm sorry. I know you don't understand. But this is the first break we've had. I believe the man you were in bed with last night is a serial killer. Somewhere, locked up in your consciousness is the information we need to catch him."

Raven got up from her seat so fast her chair fell backward to the floor. Nugent, who had been squatting in front of her, tumbled backward, sprawling on the floor. He struck his head on the edge of Wolfgang's desk. Exasperated, a gasp of pain flew from his mouth. He rubbed his head while climbing to his feet.

Raven's eyes sprayed bullets at Wolfgang. She set her legs apart in a combative stance. She pointed a finger directly in Wolfgang's face. "For the last time. The man I was in bed with last night was Micah Jordan-Wells. And for the record, he is not a murderer." She locked gazes with Wolfgang, looking supremely confident and sure of her position.

Wolfgang only nodded. His decision had been made.

Chapter 29

Later in the evening Wolfgang and Nugent stood in front of City Hall. They were in a huddle. They watched the passing traffic.

Wolfgang pulled his collar close around his neck. The night air was brisk. He eyed Nugent before speaking. Finally he said, "Nugent, I have to ask you a question I'm not happy with."

Nugent appeared distracted and said, "Shoot."

Wolfgang turned to him. "I know you usually stay all night with Micah. Were you in the office with him the entire night last night?"

Nugent was back in focus now. He turned away from the burning heat of Wolfgang's eyes. "What kind of crazy-ass question is that?"

Wolfgang swallowed hard. "It's a direct question, Nugent. Were you with Micah all night long?"

Nugent was evasive. He shifted uneasily. "I might have left for a little while." He walked away, but Wolfgang put out a hand to stop him.

"What do you mean by a little while, Nugent?"

Nugent stopped walking. He faced Wolfgang, "I don't know exactly, Wolfgang."

Wolfgang stepped closer to Nugent. He grabbed him by the shoulders. "Micah is like a son to me, Nugent. He *is* the homicide department. He holds the most convictions in the history of this department."

"He is the brightest, smartest, toughest detective Newark has ever seen. This is serious business. Now I'm going to ask you again. Exactly how much of a little while is a little while?" Wolfgang gritted his teeth. He waited for Nugent's answer.

Nugent summoned everything he had to stay in control. Wolfgang didn't miss a twitch. "I didn't stay all night. I was feeling burned out. I came back this morning. Is that what you wanted to hear?"

Wolfgang let go of Nugent. Pure weariness was etched into his voice. "As a matter of fact, it isn't. I'm getting worried, Nugent. Lately Micah doesn't seem to be where people think he is. The evidence is stacking up against him."

"Micah was in the office all night last night, Wolfgang," Nugent said testily.

Wolfgang shot back, "How do you know? You weren't there."

"If you'd seen his face when Raven stated he was with her last night, you'd know damn well he wasn't in bed with her, Wolfgang. If he's telling the truth about that, then he's telling the truth about the rest. Raven may very well be the only answer."

Wolfgang looked up at the sky as though the answer to all his problems was written there. He closed his eyes in contemplation, and said, "Okay. Maybe Raven's all we've got. Maybe she's all we need."

"The killer has made his first real mistake, Wolfgang. By sleeping with Raven Oliver."

Micah Jordan-Wells stood across the street from City Hall in the shadows of the alleyway. He watched Wolfgang and Nugent talking.

Darkness descended on the city of Newark. Micah stared down at the ground. A molten "X" in flaming fire appeared before his eyes. A spasm passed through his body. Micah shook uncontrollably.

Standing behind Micah in the shadows was Quentin Curry. Light streamed from his eyes. He whispered, "Welcome to my world, Micah. Come to me, little boy."

Micah stood stock-still. He was not aware of Quentin's presence. He continued to stare across the street at Wolfgang and Nugent.

A light emitted from his eyes. The pounding in his head started once again. He grabbed his head as though somehow he could stop the searing pain.

Chapter 30

The following morning some kids were cutting through the alley-way across the street from City Hall. One of them screamed. The others stopped to see what was going on.

Once the horror of what they were looking at sunk in, the screaming broke out in unison. A collective high-pitched wail erupted from their throats as though being conducted by an unseen director.

One of the boys retched on the ground losing his breakfast. It bubbled up from his stomach landing with a splat all over the ground, covering his shoes.

On the ground was the body of a six-year-old boy. Written in blood on the ground was the symbol of an "X." Below that, in blood, it read, "X was here."

The boy's body was nude. It was the same pattern as all the others. The child lay in his own urine and feces. His body was drenched in blood. The carving of an "X" had split open the middle of his chest.

His arms and legs were spread-eagled, nailed to pieces of wood. His eyes stared at the early morning sky. They were filmed over with a glaze that enhanced the petrified look in them.

Rigid eternity glared from the fixed pupils. The child's expression was one of scathing horrid fear. The fear was so cloying it hung in the air.

The nails in the child's body were rusty, ragged and much too large for the size of the child's hands and legs. They had torn and ripped the skin, leaving a trail of ragged, jagged skin, ripped and torn with blood trailing out.

A foamy white creamy substance streamed from the boy's lips. The child's mouth was thrown open as though a desperate plea were trying to escape it and it had gotten strangled in the creamy white substance.

Wolfgang hung up the phone. He looked at Nugent. Nugent stood tensely in the doorway of Wolfgang's office. "Another boy has been found, right in our own backyard, across the street from City Hall. It's the same M.O. Although, the usual message, 'What is the tie that binds?' is missing."

Wolfgang stuck his hands in his pockets. He went to the window and stared out wondering how many times he had made this same journey from his desk to the window. It was becoming a familiar pattern.

At the offices of the New Jersey Institute for Living, Derrick Holt was talking to one of the office clerks. She shook her head at Derrick. "I can't help you. I'm sorry."

"Well thanks for your assistance," Derrick told her. He left the office. He was determined, yet disappointment flashed across his face.

Outside, Derrick spotted an old man. He watched the old man. He seemed to be about seventy-five years old. He was the maintenance man for the institution.

The old man had the wizened look of someone who had seen everything. Excitement coursed through Derrick's veins as an idea developed.

He walked up to the man and introduced himself, "Excuse me, sir." The old man stopped raking the leaves to look at Derrick. Derrick stuck out his hand in a warm and friendly manner. "I'm Derrick Holt from the *Star-Ledger* newspaper."

The old man wiped his hands on his overalls and reached to shake Derrick's hand. "Nice to meet you. I'm William Broughton." William was glad to see a friendly face. Sometimes working at the institution was very lonely for him.

Encouraged by the maintenance man's warm manner, Derrick decided to take a chance. "How long have you worked here?" he asked William.

William scrunched his eyes in thought, "About forty years."

Derrick brightened at his answer. He took a flying leap in pursuit of his goal. "So you knew Silky? He probably went by the name of David Edward Stokes when he was here."

William smiled a toothy grin. Derrick knew he had hit pay dirt.

"Knew him and the other one. Things about them that you wouldn't believe though. Strange things."

Derrick was taken aback at his answer. "The other one? What other one?"

William raked the leaves so he could look busy and not like he was just gabbing. "Him and the one named Shaughn Braswell. Whew!"

Derrick watched him work, mesmerized with his good fortune.

William wiped a hand across his brow. "I'll tell you they were something. They used to conduct some kind of rituals." He paused for a moment to catch his breath. "Unspeakable things. Ugly things. Pure evil. Messing with things people shouldn't be messing with. Stirring up bad spirits. It wasn't pretty, I tell ya. It was a rare day the reverend ever left his knees at the altar in the chapel when them two was here. Had to pray them bad spirits away."

He pointed to a basement window in the institution. "Right over there." He stopped raking to look at Derrick. "Of course, you learn over the years to keep your mouth shut in these places about things. Everybody has something to hide. So many secrets, you know."

William rambled, "I can't say these people haven't been good to me. I'm seventy-five years old, should have been gone long ago, but they been keeping me on, continuing to let me work. I've got to work you know. When you get to be my age, if you don't work, you die."

Derrick nodded. "At your age you should be enjoying some of the finer things in life too, William." Derrick pulled three crisp one-hundred dollar bills from his pocket. He slipped them to William. "I'd like to talk about Silky and Shaughn's stay here."

William accepted the bills. They walked across the manicured, leaf-strewn ground as William narrated the story of Silky and Shaughn for Derrick.

William's sense of loneliness had faded for the time. He was animated with sharing information from the past. The past was where he lived most of the time these days.

The past was also where some of the darkest of his memories were buried. This particular memory had been tucked away behind a curtain in his mind, not to be retrieved until now.

They walked over to the basement window as William Broughton led Derrick down a pathway to a dark world that hovered just outside of the natural. Occasionally there was a merger that upset the balance of things.

Later that night, Derrick was in the dark office of the New Jersey Institute. It was the same office where the clerk had refused to help him. He shined his flashlight into a broken file drawer where he had just picked the lock.

In his entire career, he had never broken and entered into anything to obtain a story, but he considered this a small breach considering what he thought he was on to.

He spotted the file he was looking for. He lifted it out of the drawer. Opening it, he reached inside to rifle through the papers. He scanned the information quickly. A surge of joy rushed through him.

Derrick pulled out a mini camera. He snapped shots in quick succession. The digital camera produced laser-quality photographs. He was euphoric. He came to a newspaper clipping. He pulled it out for closer inspection.

A long slow involuntary whistle puckered his lips.

Derrick exhaled. He felt like he had been waiting to exhale all his life. Now he knew what all those women had been so exhilarated about when the phrase "Waiting to Exhale" had been coined. Yes. It could happen to a man too.

Albeit his reasons were different.

But feel it he did. His excitement knew no bounds. He'd known all along that something wasn't right. Now he had the evidence to prove it. Although in a million years he had never expected this particular bonanza. He wouldn't have imagined this in his wildest daydreams. "I'm going to be Journalist of the Year!"

It was all he could do to keep from flipping a cartwheel. He was already picturing the sparkling award hanging in his office. Offers would pour in from all over the country when the story broke. Damned if he wouldn't be ready.

Derrick drove home. He talked into his microcassette recorder. Getting it all down. One of the first things he had learned in journalism was to always carry the tools of your trade. You never knew when something might pop up.

Derrick was a good student. He had followed this advice religiously throughout his career. He put the microcassette recorder close to his lips and said, "This exposé is hot. It is going to blow the lid off one of the most incredible, twisted cases Newark has ever seen."

He paused visualizing the headlines. He could hardly believe his good fortune.

When Derrick arrived home, he went straight to his desk. He pored over his notes. He flipped through his files. He knew he had finally hit on the truth surrounding Silky. What an incredible truth it was.

Silky and Shaughn. There was no doubt after what he'd discovered that Shaughn was part of the killings, both then and now. He had known Silky's story didn't stop there, that there was more to it, that Silky was somehow affiliated with the occult. The murders of the women had smacked of it and so had Silky's strange death.

People always said that *the truth* was stranger than fiction. Here he sat with the perfect specimen of the popular myth.

The story was so explosive he knew it was going to rip Newark open to its very core. It would blow away the very foundation of Newark. This was absolutely the mother ship of all stories. Derrick slapped his forehead. He just couldn't believe it.

Shivering with excitement, Derrick booted up his computer. He gleefully typed in a draft of what his headline would be.

"Damn," he said as he looked at the headline he'd typed. "Pulitzer Prize material." His daydream ran rampant. The bold black letters leaped from the computer before his eyes. He could hardly wait to see the expression on Chris White's face when he told him. The sweet smell of being right was making him dizzy.

"Now Wolfgang and Micah will come face-to-face with the truth. And we'll see what they have to say about this. Oh, what a day it will be." Derrick smiled.

He thumbed his nose at an imaginary Micah. He recalled Micah's words, "There is no story. Period. Now go find some real work to do." Derrick's eyes shone brighter than the light on the computer.

"No story, huh? I wonder what you'd call *this*, Micah."

He leaned back in his chair. He jiggled the toothpick from side to side, unaware he was being watched and of the threat his newfound information posed. He heard a whooshing sound behind him.

Derrick turned in shocked surprise to see a flaming ball of fire heading toward him with the speed of light. In an instant Derrick was engulfed in flames. He turned into a human fireball. His screams of anguish bounced and then echoed off the walls.

The flames licked slowly away at everything in the room. His research, his camera, and his computer melted in the molten heat of the fire.

The fire licked its way over to the microcassette recorder. It left nothing in its wake but ashes.

Chapter 31

Micah stood in the hall outside of Patrick Hayes's office. Patrick was forty years old. He was hands down one of the hottest DAs on the East Coast.

He rose to shake hands with Micah as he entered the office. "Micah. Please have a seat," Patrick told him. "It's good to see you."

Once Micah was seated Patrick took his seat behind the desk.

"It's good to see you too, Patrick," Micah replied.

Patrick smiled. He had always liked Micah. His manner was forthright. He had a strong sense of fair play. Those were qualities Patrick respected and admired. Micah was a man who could be trusted. Not to mention one hell of a detective. They had danced together on a tightrope in their case against Silky and won.

"So, what brings you here?"

"Do you still have the psyche report on Silky?"

Patrick gave him a strange look. "Silky's dead."

"Yeah I know but I'm playing the hunch so humor me."

Patrick knew it was more than that but he didn't question it further. "Yeah, I've got the report."

"Patrick, let's go over Silky's psyche."

Patrick looked at Micah before replying, "You know he was the devil's watchdog. Automated and programmed."

Patrick picked up a computer disk from his desk. He twirled it in his fingers. "Just like this disk. What you put in is what you get out."

Micah didn't say a word.

"The problem is, Micah, you're talking about mind control. You know as well as I do the medical community doesn't totally accept it. But it happens." Patrick looked past Micah, momentarily. "This case crossed the realm. David Edward Stokes was possessed. He wasn't an ordinary criminal by any means, you know that."

Patrick sensed Micah's uneasiness but he continued on. "There were things about the murders that were inconsistent with other murders of this type. I still have the report."

"What do you mean by inconsistent, Patrick?"

"Remember the markings?"

Micah seized on a moment of insight as the image of the marking parked itself in his mind's eye.

Patrick flashed Micah a look. "All of the victims had the number six embedded into the base of their skulls. Just above the neck area. Barely visible to the human eye." Patrick cleared his throat.

"When David was interviewed he claimed the women he killed were carriers. He said they were carriers of a mark from God. Carriers of a seed that would rise up and fight against the seed of Satan."

"He said that was why they needed to be destroyed. He claimed the seeds of the chosen ones were here. Here in Newark. Who knows what he meant? He ranted on and on about how Satan had been tricked because the women were carriers of the mark but would never produce the seeds of the chosen ones."

In a flash of insight Micah suddenly realized an elaborate plan of deceit had taken place. The chosen ones were not born of the mur- dered women. These women had the ability to produce but the boys they had born did not bear the mark. The ones that were being killed now did.

A tremor shook Micah's body. Shadowy images of the murdered women branded with an "X" rose from his consciousness. The six- year-old boys floated before his eyes.

Trying to gather himself Micah asked, "What did the report say about Silky's parents?"

"It said he was an orphan. He was picked up by Child Protective Services while wandering the streets of Newark when he was . . ."

Patrick paused trying to recall. "When he was six. David Stokes was raised by the State of New Jersey at The New Jersey Institute of Living. The address of the institution is right here."

A seed of truth dropped in Micah's lap. The stench of deceit clogged his nostrils. Micah switched gears.

"Just one question, Patrick." Before Micah could ask the question, his body began to quiver strangely. Patrick's face was replaced by a molten "X" melting and dripping in flames.

Micah was tossed into a room. Derrick Holt was engulfed in flames. Derrick's screams of anguish bounced, and then echoed off the walls. Over in a corner of the room, a silhouette moved. Micah was face to face with his own shadow. He smiled at himself. Derrick was dead. So was the secret. It had died with him.

Chapter 32

Micah sat on the edge of his bed listening to the news on the radio. The announcer's voice was like a cold blast of air in his ear. "A fire in Newark today claimed the life of the *Star-Ledger*'s news reporter, Derrick Holt. A top-notch reporter, Derrick was noted for his outstanding journalism in the field of criminology. The origin of the fire is at this time unknown."

Micah closed his eyes. The phone rang. It rang and rang. Finally, he lifted the receiver. "Micah Jordan-Wells, here."

"Micah, is everything okay?" Evelyn said. Her voice was laced with something unrecognizable. It went over Micah's head. "I've been worried about you."

"You shouldn't be worried about me, Ma. You should be writing your next book." Micah was careful to keep the strain out of his voice. He knew Evelyn was not good with trauma or stressful situations.

In her parlor, Evelyn peeked again out the window from behind the heavy brocade drapes. She saw the reverend across the street watching her house. She took a sip from her coffee cup. The reverend beckoned to her. Quickly she pulled back from the window.

"Well, I'm doing that too, Micah. But I still find time to worry. I know you don't like to discuss your cases. But, please. Be careful. I don't like the sound of this one." This statement was a major milestone for Evelyn. It was as far as she could bring herself to go.

The beautiful glass figurine flung itself from the table, shattering in tiny, colorful pieces. Except for the neck. The slender neck of the figurine was broken in half. Evelyn fought to keep her calm. Micah must not know.

"I'll be careful, Ma. Don't worry. I'll be by there soon. Okay?"

Evelyn forced a calmness she didn't feel into her voice. "Of course darling. You know I'll be here."

A snappy tone edged into Micah's voice. He couldn't help it. Evelyn simply exasperated him at times with the way she ran away from things. "I wish you wouldn't be there, Ma. You should be out having live book signings or something. Your fans should be able to see you in person, not just in pictures and via video tapings. I still don't know why you write under the name Blaine Upshaw anyway. You should be proud of what you do. Why are you writing under a pseudonym?"

Evelyn frowned. She sucked in a space of air. She was a bit taken aback by Micah's blunt question. He generally handled her with kid gloves. She had come to expect this gentle treatment from him. He had spoiled her in many aspects by catering to her idiosyncrasies. Now, just when she didn't need it, he was intruding on things better left alone.

What Evelyn didn't realize was that Micah had had about as much secrecy as he could bear. He was slowly sliding off the edge.

When she answered, Evelyn's tone had a bit of snap in it as well. "Listen, Micah, do not start this. I didn't call to fight. I just missed you. There are things in life better off left alone."

Evelyn's nerves were frayed around the edges. If there was ever a time she didn't want to explain this to Micah, now was it. She drained her coffee cup.

"Yeah, I know. You've always told me that. I love you, Ma," Micah answered.

Evelyn risked another look out the drapes. She saw that the reverend was gone. She sat down. She looked at the glass figurine. Its neck was broken. She clasped her shaking hands in her lap. "I love you, baby. More than you know." Softly she hung up the phone.

She saw Quentin force her face up to his. His gaze bore into her. His words echoed in the chambers of her ears. "If you ever try to leave you will die! You will die a death more vicious than the wildest imagination can conjure up.

"Painfully and slowly, I will release life from your body. Until you beg for death. Until you seek its face. I will kill you and anything you love. Understood? Look at the mark." The "X" swam before her eyes like a watery illusion.

Evelyn put her head in her hands and wept. If she tried to protect Micah he would die. Weeping Willow sank down on the sofa. She looked at the woman sitting before her, and she too wept.

Micah heard the soft click of the phone in his ear. He decided to call Nugent. He listened to the ringing until Nugent's voice came over the phone. "Nuggie, how's Raven?"

Micah listened to Nugent's reply and said, "Listen, I can't deal with this right now. Just make sure she's in good hands for me. Tell her I still love her." Micah's voice broke on the last words as he examined the ruins of his manhood.

His ego had been badly damaged by another man making love to his woman. Micah twisted the phone cord tight around his whitened knuckles. He spat out his next words. "He slept with her, man. Can you believe this? This is bull crap, Nugent. Are you getting me? She thought it was me. It wasn't, Nugent. You know damn well it wasn't me. He went too far this time. I'm gonna rip this punk to shreds when I find him. How the hell could she have thought it was me? That's impossible. I've been with Raven for five years. She knows me. How in the hell could she have thought it was me? He touched her. She made love to another man, and she thought it was me!"

Micah had finally voiced the one fear that wouldn't leave him alone. The one thought that always nagged him. It vanquished his sleep. He couldn't escape it. *How in the hell could somebody be him, unless it was him?*

The murders always came to him in visions. Flashes of what would be, of what was. Only, he had finally seen himself in Derrick's apartment. Face to face.

A frustrated storm raged through his body. He threw the telephone against the wall, not bothering to finish his conversation with Nugent.

Nugent, who had been standing with the phone to his ear, heard the crash. He pulled the phone away from his ear. He listened at a distance. When he realized Micah wasn't coming back, he hung up.

Micah put his head between his knees. His head was beginning to hurt again. If only he could remember what happened.

After a time, Micah opened the drawer to the nightstand. He pulled out a bottle of Hennessey. He swigged the cognac, taking deep swallows.

He stared at the bottle in his hand while the alcohol burned its way down his throat. The bottle exploded in a ball of fire. He jumped up and stomped on the burning bottle.

Recognition seized him, sweeping him off his feet. This couldn't be possible. But it was. He focused on different objects in the room, realizing his newfound power. Coming into a gift so profound it rocked his world.

He stared at objects, discovering he had the ability to move them and float them at will. If he stared intently, they burst into flames. He also discovered the ability to quench the flames. If he moderated his stare, he could move, float, or destroy the object, depending on his level of intensity.

He restored everything he experimented on to its rightful state and place. Then he sat down on the edge of his bed trying to come to grips with what he was.

Had he been hunting himself all along?

The thought of it made his insides heave. He'd thought it was just some kind of sick joke. Although, he still hadn't figured out how people kept thinking he was in places he wasn't. At least he didn't remember being there until they floated back to him in images.

Micah stared at the wall. Realization, the awful truth of what he was, gripped him in a steel-like vise. Once more, the molten "X" burned itself into the wall.

Shrieks of insane laughter came at him from out of the wall. The shrieking surrounded him now. The banshees wailed. Micah's entrée into a different world was upon him. He was welcomed.

Micah twirled around. He grabbed his head. The shrieking laughter grew louder. He felt a presence in the room. Quentin Curry stood before him.

Micah blinked. "Where the hell did you come from? How did you get in here? Who are you?"

Quentin laughed. "Who I am doesn't matter. It's who you are that matters, Micah. You're demon spawn."

Micah lunged at Quentin and came up with air. Quentin was behind him, laughing at him. Micah was so very tired of living with this insane laughter. He whirled on Quentin. He would rip him to pieces with his bare hands. But Quentin disappeared. "No!" Micah shouted at him.

The laughter stopped as quickly as it began. Quentin's words were all that were left in the room. "Yes," he said. "Oh, yes, Micah Jordan-Wells."

Over in a corner of the room Weeping Willow stood with her arms outstretched to Micah. Tears streamed from her eyes. They rolled down her cheeks.

Before Micah's eyes, she knelt in a state of repentance.

Chapter 33

The reverend lay in his bed as Quentin Curry silently slipped into the bedroom. He crept to the reverend's bed, watching his sleeping form. He had originally thought the reverend might add a bit of an edge to things, something he would enjoy, but now the reverend's meddling was getting out of hand.

The reverend hadn't posed much of a problem in the early days. But since the murders started, his concern with Micah had escalated. Now the reverend was becoming a liability Quentin could no longer afford. As such, he simply had to be eliminated.

Quentin stared at the sleeping figure. He blinked his eyes, emitting light in a stream toward the reverend.

The bolt of light struck the bedpost. It bounced back. Quentin frowned in surprise. He tried again. The reverend should be an easy target for him. He didn't tolerate opposition. Again, the stream of light struck the bedpost without touching the reverend.

Quentin didn't have time for playing games. There was work to be done. He mustered his supreme power. Screeching from the depths of hell broke out in the room. The level of darkness deepened to an unholy degree.

Quentin's eyes gleamed with a force that rocked the very foundation of the reverend's house. The house shook from the force of it. He rooted the house up out of the ground leaving a gaping hole.

The house soared through the atmosphere. Tiles rained down from the roof. Another bolt of light streamed from his eyes directly at the reverend's heart.

An authoritative energy blocked the bolt. A golden light circled the reverend's bed rendering it untouchable.

Quentin was furious.

The house soared through the air at a greater speed. The doors slammed. The windows blew out. He hurled a chair at the reverend's head. It crashed against the wall, never touching him. A wind of tornado-like proportions blew through the room, intent on sucking the reverend into its vortex.

It would suck the reverend and his house into oblivion. The tornado whirled right past the reverend. It hurled itself out the back bedroom window.

Quentin spat fireballs at the reverend from his eyes. A golden circle absorbed the balls of fire like a sponge. He threw a shroud of darkness, the net of his kingdom, at the reverend. There were very few men who had ever escaped it. The shroud dissolved.

The old cross made of tree bark fell from the wall. A blue streak of lightning burst forth from the cross. Thunder rolled, rocking the room. The cross was stained with a dark red substance. Blood. Underneath the cross a pool of blood seeped into the carpet. It was the blood of the slain.

The collection of Bibles were hewn from their shelves, they pummeled Quentin. The word assaulted him. Quentin screeched in abject fear. A howl rose from his throat. Pure, unadulterated fear racked his body.

Before his eyes the rock-hewn churches of Ethiopia rose out of their depths. They surrounded him, a circle of holiness and deep empowering faith. Housed in a shrine in one of the churches were the Ten Commandments.

A man dressed in heavy black winter clothing with a derby stuck on his head rose up before Quentin. He spoke one word. "Go!"

Quentin backed away from the reverend. He backed away from the cross. The blood was still seeping. *Please. Don't let it touch me.* There was a flapping sound. The flapping of thousands of wings sounded throughout the bedroom, rising in crescendo. The screeching came to an immediate halt. A holy army had arrived.

Quentin backed out of the room. He backed into the hallway. The room was bathed in a soft golden light. The door slammed in his face.

The house settled. It was restored to its rightful foundation. An angel of wrath guarded the door. Quentin knew him. He wielded supreme power. The blue-white mist of a spirit settled itself before the door.

Quentin couldn't believe it. There were very few of these idiots who ever tapped into that power. Apparently the reverend had. The reverend had discovered the ultimate weapon. He believed. And he had seized hold of the only power that could force this snake, raised out of the pit, back into its place

Quentin had underestimated the reverend. He remembered a time when the reverend had shook at the sight of him. "Damn him," Quentin said.

But he knew his words were without effect or power. The reverend had risen to the occasion. He had connected to The Lord Jesus Christ! The King of Kings! The King of Glory!

Quentin was pissed. It didn't matter. The reverend was protected. And he couldn't touch him. He had no choice but to back off. He would have to chalk the Reverend Erwin Jackson up as a loss. Quentin took one last angry look at the door, swept his hands in the air and disappeared.

Inside the bedroom, the reverend lay on his side in the bed. He clutched his tree bark cross. There were only four of them in the world. He had been graced to be the owner of three. One of which he had given to Micah Jordan-Wells.

He prayed softly under his breath, "He that is in me is greater than he that is in the world. He that is in me is greater than he that is in the world."

He looked up from his prayer to see the silhouettes of angels rising upwards.

"Thank you, Jesus," he said. "Thank you, Lord."

Chapter 34

Nugent studied the map of Newark that was posted on the wall. Red and green pushpins had been arranged so that they formed an "X" across the city of Newark. Each pushpin represented the location of one of the murder victims, starting back with Silky's reign.

Next to the map was a series of pictures. The latest victim had found his place on the wall. Nugent zoomed in on the faces. Files were strewn all over the desk.

He reached for his bottle of root beer. He took a long swallow. Gaddy came in carrying a tray filled with doughnuts, pastries, and half sandwiches. He sat the tray on the table.

"Here, Nugent. This all-night thing is like a stakeout. It's not all that. Know what I mean? I brought you some grub. If you can't feed the spirit, you can at lest feed the flesh." Nugent gratefully reached for a sandwich. He stuffed it in his mouth.

Wolfgang walked in. He spied the tray. "You're a good man, Gaddy."

Gaddy smiled. "Naw, a brother's just got to do what a brother's got to do. Besides, there's no laughter around here no more, man. Maybe, if I keep a brother fed, things will return to normal. Lighten up a bit." Gaddy walked out of the office closing the door behind him.

Wolfgang took in all the files scattered on the desk. He gazed at the map. Blood rushed through his face.

"Wolfgang, Micah was on the track. It's paying off." Nugent pointed to the map.

"The green pins represent the location of the women's bodies. Silky crisscrossed the city. The murders of the boys and the women are linked."

Wolfgang studied the map, "So, Silky was representing Criss Cross all along."

Nugent sighed, "Exactly."

Excitedly, Nugent walked over to the computer. Wolfgang was right behind him. The computer screen was flashing the name of David Edward Stokes in red text. Underneath the name, the word "Confidential" was written. Nugent pointed to the screen.

"That's Silky's file from the institution where he grew up. I accessed it." Wolfgang declined to comment on Nugent's hacking skills.

"Silky was an orphan like Micah suspected. Institutionalized at age six. His mother set him outdoors one day. Told him she couldn't afford him, so keep stepping. I guess it was too expensive to feed Silky along with a heroin habit."

"Nice lady," Wolfgang replied.

Nugent said, "Derrick Holt was researching a piece on Silky. His charred remains have been matched and identified from his dental charts. I'm not saying his death is connected. But if it is, we're closer than we think. Somebody is getting paranoid."

Wolfgang looked at him. "Do you think Derrick found the information?"

"I think it's a distinct possibility. What if he found it and the killer murdered him? We'd better have another talk with Raven. I really think she may be our only shot."

Wolfgang entwined his fingers. "Silky's fingerprints are missing from our files."

Nugent raised a surprised eyebrow but stood his ground. "I don't care. Silky's actual fingertips were missing from the jail files, too. Hell, Silky didn't have his own fingerprints for who knows how long."

"Micah is not committing these murders, Wolfgang. I don't care what it looks like. We're dealing with a psychopath who thinks he's

God. And somehow he is impersonating Micah. The rules are different."

The two men locked gazes.

"You realize my entire career is on the line here, Nugent. By right I should have pulled Micah's badge until this was sorted out. If it should leak out that Micah was a suspect and I kept him on the case, the media will crucify me, and my career will be in the toilet."

"If I'm wrong I'll toss mine in the toilet with yours. But I don't think I am. Deep inside, neither do you, Wolfgang. If you did, you wouldn't have held on this long."

Wolfgang sat down heavily on the edge of the desk. For the first time in his career, his fifty years were showing. "If we're right on this and it's not Micah, then I hope you'll never tell another soul we had this conversation."

Nugent put a hand on Wolfgang's shoulder. He nodded.

Wolfgang studied him carefully. He knew the words would never leave Nugent's lips in this lifetime.

Shortly thereafter, Raven was seated next to Nugent in Wolfgang's office. Nugent patted her hand.

She had been held by Wolfgang and questioned repeatedly while in special holding. But now Wolfgang had reached his decision. So he said, "Raven, I know this has been a difficult time for you. But I need you to agree to undergo hypnosis. It has to be off the record."

Raven frowned. She was growing weary of what she considered their browbeating. She wanted to get this over with. She needed to get on with her life.

They had tried their best to make her as comfortable as possible in the situation. But her nerves were shot to hell. Her patience was frayed to the breaking point. She didn't understand how they could think she was not with Micah, when she had told them time and time again that she was.

She looked at Wolfgang. "Why? Why do you need me to undergo hypnosis?"

"Because you love Micah. So do I. So does Nugent. I believe hypnosis is the only way to break through and unlock your impressions from that night. You'll never remember on your own. You're too convinced about it."

Damn straight I am. Who the hell else would I have been in bed with? She bit her tongue to keep from spitting the words in Wolfgang's face.

Nugent said, "You'll have to trust us, Raven. We need to prove once and for all that the man people keep thinking is Micah, is not. If you went to bed with him, that means he looks, sounds and acts exactly like Micah, but he's not.

"Don't ask me how, because I don't know. But I do know we have to prove somebody is framing Micah. You're the only one who can do that without sending out alarms that we don't want ringing. He looks like Micah. He acts like Micah. Apparently. But he's not. So, there must be a way to prove it. Something about him has to be different. We need to find out what it is."

Nugent took Raven by the shoulders and looked deep in her eyes, "Raven, I don't know what's going on. But whatever it is, it's not normal. That means we can't think normal. The hypnosis has got to be confidential. It's got to be off the record. And it needs to happen now. You have to trust us."

"Why? Why should I trust you?"

Wolfgang came over and pulled Raven to her feet. He stared deep into her eyes, before playing his ace card. "Because I think you slept with the real killer. And we never want it to leave the walls of this office that at any time, Micah could possibly have ever been a suspect."

Wolfgang sighed before continuing. "Because I am hiding an eyewitness who gave a positive ID on Micah being the killer. Because Micah can't prove his whereabouts at the time of the murder. Because there can't be any doubt as to Micah's innocence. Do you want there to be any doubt, Raven?"

Raven pulled her eyes away from the pain in Wolfgang's eyes. She spoke softly, "No."

Wolfgang nodded. "Good. I know someone who can perform the hypnosis."

Chapter 35

Inside Justin Rivers's living room that night Raven lay back on a sofa propped up on pillows. Justin was the East Coast's leading criminal psychologist. The room was warm and inviting. The color scheme was muted and unobtrusive. The soothing sounds of waves on the ocean were barely discernible in the background.

Justin didn't hesitate; once Wolfgang outlined the situation for him.

Some of Justin's hypnosis cases had become case studies for psychologists all over the country. If anyone could get at the answers, he was the man. And he was familiar with the case having done the psyche evaluation on David Edward Stokes.

Justin looked at Raven. Her breathing was steady and even. Her eyes were closed. She was in a relaxed state of mind. This was good. It was exactly where Justin needed her to be.

Wolfgang and Nugent hovered anxiously in the background. Justin spoke to Raven softly, "Raven, just relax. We're all friends here. Tell me where you are."

"I'm in Maroon's with Micah."

"What did you have for dinner?"

Raven smiled. "We had red snapper and macaroni and cheese with collard greens."

Justin nodded. "Whose idea was it to have red snapper for dinner?"

"Micah suggested it. He loves red snapper, and so do I."

"Did you have anything to drink?"

"Yes. We had a bottle of Möet."

"Why? Were you celebrating?"

"No. Well, I don't know. Maybe. In a way, I guess. We drink Möet sometimes when we haven't had much time together. I guess we sort of celebrate our time together."

"Why were you at the restaurant?"

"Micah called. He invited me."

"Is there anyone else who knows he invited you?"

"Yes. Brandi."

"Was music playing in the restaurant?"

A slight frown creased Raven's brow. Then she smiled in remembrance. "Yes. Brian McKnight's song was playing. You know the one. It says, One, you're like a dream come true. Two, just wanna be with you. Umm, I think the name is 'Back at One.' Yes. That's it. 'Back at One.'"

Justin said, "It sounds like you had a good time."

Dreamily, Raven replied, "Yeah. We did."

Justin decided it was time to switch gears. "Tell me Raven. What is Micah doing?"

"He's looking at me."

"Is there anything different about him?"

"No. He's just as fine as always."

Justin smiled. "Did he touch you?"

"Yes."

"Where?"

"He . . . He . . ." Raven frowned. She moaned. Blinking, her body surged forward. Suddenly her entire body heaved. The word "No" spilled out of her lips. A tense cord of anticipation permeated the air.

Wolfgang and Nugent craned their necks to get a closer look at Raven. Nugent balled his hand into a tight fist.

Justin held up a hand to Wolfgang and Nugent to ensure their silence.

Without breaking stride, soothingly Justin spoke to Raven, "What Raven? What is it? Tell me what you see."

"My hair. Micah pushed my hair behind my ear." Raven sees them in Maroon's. She sees Shaughn smooth back a lock of her hair. She smiles, but when he draws his hand back Raven looks down, noticing something peculiar.

Hysterical, blood-curdling screams erupted from her mouth, shattering the silence in the room. On the back of Shaughn's right hand was a mark. It was barely discernible, faint, but nevertheless there. A molten "X" was embedded in the skin.

Wolfgang, Nugent, and Justin watched Raven anxiously. Wolfgang started to worry because Raven was thrashing around on the couch. He didn't want her to disconnect from them. He didn't want her stuck in that time, in that place. She was writhing around as though she were in pain.

Wolfgang whispered harshly, "Bring her out. Bring her out, now."

Justin refused his request. He had to. He was the professional. He knew Wolfgang was speaking from emotion. They couldn't afford it. "No. Wait. She has the answer."

Raven let out a shrill cry, "No! There's an 'X' on the back of his right hand. Micah doesn't have a mark on his hand."

Raven looked back into Shaughn's eyes. She was staring into a void. There was nothing there. Absolutely nothing. Why hadn't she noticed before?

Micah's eyes flashed warmth and compassion. The man sitting before her was a shell of Micah. He was an illusion. Hell, he was a monster. He was not Micah. The instant the realization hit her, Raven's world came crashing down around her.

She was swimming in a dark haze. Waves of black washed over her. She tried to get back to shore. She tried to swim back to the anchor of Justin and Wolfgang. She choked and sputtered in the process.

Shaughn grabbed her. "You're mine, now."

Raven fought him like a wildcat. "The hell I am!" She kicked wildly. She focused on Justin's living room. All she had to do was get there. Someone was laughing. Lunatic laughter exploded around her. Raven ignored it. She focused.

The three men exchanged looks. They didn't move. They didn't dare to even breathe.

Justin held out his hand. Like the director of an orchestra, not one note of the symphony would change until he directed it to do so.

He looked at Raven allowing her to swim through her emotions before bringing her back. Allowing her to fight back. It was crucial to her survival. She must achieve this by her own will. She needed to come face to face with her own soul.

An additional second passed. Justin snapped his fingers three times. He brought Raven out from under the hypnosis. Raven sat up. She was still crying. Deep sobs racked her body. She slid her legs off the couch. She accepted the tissue Justin handed her.

"Oh God. No wonder he hates me. Oh, God, Wolfgang. It wasn't Micah. He . . . he . . . he touched me. He looks, acts, and sounds like Micah. Only . . . when you look into his eyes, there's no one there. It isn't him. My God, Wolfgang, this man is not Micah!"

Raven was bordering on the edge of hysteria. She put her head in her hands. She whimpered and moaned in pain. Finally, she looked up. She shook her head amazed at the sheer incredibility of it all.

Three pairs of eyes watched her. Focusing, she said, "It wasn't Micah. I made love to another man. I . . . I let him touch me. He looked like Micah. He smelled like Micah. He even . . . he even moves like Micah . . . How in the hell can somebody else look and be exactly like Micah?"

All of them exchanged looks. The question hung in the air.

Wolfgang felt a swell of relief. Yet he knew they were not all the way home yet. Taking Raven's hand in his, he said, "I don't know, Raven. But we're going to find out. Count on it. By the way, Nugent talked to Micah. He still loves you. He said it's going to be all right."

Wolfgang stepped out and embellished a little bit. He wanted to help Raven feel a little better. "He also said he's sorry he snapped at you. He just needs time to deal with this. Okay?"

Raven nodded. She attempted a smile.

Nugent's mind was running in circles. He'd known there was no way Micah could be the killer.

"If someone is committing murders and passing himself off as Micah, this presents a strange twist. I witnessed a psychotic episode with Micah," Justin said. "He came to the office after a visit with Patrick."

Justin pursed his lips in thought. He knew he was about to reach. But there was nothing about this case that didn't require looking at the bizarre.

Edging forward on the theory taking shape in his mind he said,

"This reminds me of an ancient spiritual ritual where kindred spirits, so to speak, merge into one spirit. The myth being the power of the spirit grows, from the merger. It's called twinning."

"Twinning?" Wolfgang said.

"Yes. Twinning. The problem is that at the end there can only be one body in which to house that spirit. Which means somebody has got to die. The control of one mind, body, and spirit. That is what twinning is all about."

Nugent watched Justin strangely. The episode on the street when Micah appeared to be someone else flashed before his eyes. Once. Twice. "The other day on the street Micah knew that another boy had been abducted, but what was stranger than that, was that for a moment he seemed to black out. Know what I mean?"

"No," Justin said. "Explain it to me."

Nugent got up. He paced the room. The other three didn't take their eyes off of him. They didn't make a sound. No one wanted to interrupt his thoughts.

"Man, look. I don't believe in a lot of hocus-pocus. However, it was like somebody took over Micah's body. Like he wasn't even there. A voice that was not his spoke through his mouth. It said, 'When the seed of my enemy is removed all that will remain is for my seed to rule. The sixes and their carriers will be no more.' It was stranger than hell."

A ripple of acknowledgment gripped Justin.

He was on his feet. He gave Nugent a deadly serious look. "That's what David said about the dead women. He believed he was a disciple of Satan. His job was to murder the women who were carriers."

Justin paced the room following the well-worn pattern that Nugent had set. "I remember David's view was well publicized after he scared one of his cell mates by sharing this theory. It set off a ripple effect you guys must have felt the backsplash from that."

Wolfgang nodded suddenly recalling the episode.

"He said Satan got tricked because they were carriers, but they did not produce the seeds that would rise up to war with Satan. In other words, the women had children, but the children they produced weren't the chosen ones. He said the seeds were planted in Newark."

"That has to be why the boys of different women were killed," Nugent said.

Wolfgang was mesmerized. It sounded like a bad fairy tale.

However, years of training had taught him not to discount anything, no matter how strange it might seem.

And Lord knew more truths had been sprouted out through people in lockdown and in prisons than could be counted. At the time David had been looked upon as insane, and grandstanding. Now it was beginning to look like a very dark truth.

Justin continued on, "David stated that in order for them to be in a position to win the war when it takes place, Satan would need his seed to have full power. That he had to merge the powers of the flesh together. The power is being held by two separate beings. The only way for it to merge is for the two powers to twin."

Justin sat back down. He crossed his legs. He was lost in the myth. So was everyone else in the room. "Somehow, they must believe Micah is the other power. Nugent probably witnessed that spirit trying to gain control over Micah. Once they twin, it will be simple. Twinning, according to the myth, creates great power. One body will die. The other body will remain with full powers."

Justin leaned forward. The premise rolled from his tongue as full understanding kicked in. He had hit on the insights of a psychopath. Dear God.

"Twinning is the goal to reach one ultimate power. Through twinning, the spirit can keep producing itself. As it produces, it will grow in power. It believes it will generate a seed to defeat the ones marked with the mark from God. From there he can battle God directly. The seeds are the children. David believed Satan was here in the form of a man."

Raven frowned. "Dear God." A spiritual insight she didn't know she possessed seized her. The alien feeling swept through her body as though water was rushing through her veins. "They killed all those women and children in the hopes of killing off the seed before it can even be born as the chosen one to do battle, eliminating what they think is a level of power to be defeated before Satan can take over God's throne and reign?"

"Essentially," Justin said. "Although the murders are physical the twinning is a supernatural power and you can't fight in God's realm in the physical. However one can be born in the physical."

You could have heard a pin drop.

Finally Raven came forth with her last chilling thought, "What if all the murders have been for naught because he doesn't think he's gotten the chosen one yet?"

Chapter 36

Evelyn sipped from her ever-present cup of coffee. The bottle of Chivas Regal was in full view. She just didn't care. She was tired of trying to hide her pain. She was what she was. It was bigger than she was.

The evening news blared in the background. She had no interest. The newscaster's voice broke into her thoughts, penetrating her fog of disinterest. She turned at the sound of the note in the newscaster's voice.

"Another body of a six-year-old boy has been discovered. Unbelievably, the body has been found right across the street from City Hall."

An aerial shot of the area flashed across the screen. "The murders have been dubbed the Criss Cross murders. All the boy's bodies have been branded with an "X" indicating ritual-type murders."

Wolfgang had kept this out of the media as long as he could but the story had broken. Evelyn didn't hear any more. Her mind ceased functioning. Her cup slipped from her hand. It clattered to the floor. Her hands trembled. She worked her mouth. It was as dry as a cotton ball. The newscaster's voice droned in the background.

Evelyn heard a muffled sound. She ran into the foyer. She checked the locks on the door. She leaned heavily against the door, breathing deeply. She tried to steady herself so she could breathe evenly but her breath came in short rasps. She screamed out, "No!"

Evelyn slid down the length of the door. She sat on the floor, sobbing. Quentin had struck with a vengeance. He was making his ultimate move. There was no way she could stop him. His prophecy was being fulfilled. And hers had been the womb that had made it possible.

She should never have listened to Reverend Jackson so long ago. She should not have gone through with the birth. None of this would be happening now if she had gotten the abortion. Then she thought of Micah. She sobbed even louder at her loss.

Quentin's prophecy slapped her in the face with the force of a windstorm. Guilt twisted her insides into a knot. Stark fear had completely immobilized her over the years. Now it would cost her. Big time. She would pay the price for not fighting back. A price that was too big for any one person to pay.

Evelyn rolled into a fetal position on the floor. Dry sobs racked her body. She was out of tears. Sounds like that of a trapped animal with a fatal wound poured from her being.

Pain surged through her body. It swelled in her heart. A piercing arrow of grief ripped through her fear. She would lose him. If she did not make a move, Quentin would kill him.

She didn't have the courage to face him. She might not even have time on her side. But there was something she could do.

Evelyn was so immersed in fear and pain that she could not stand. Instead she crawled. Inch by inch, she crawled back to the foyer. She thought of the mural she had seen. She thought of Micah.

She dug deep. Yes, there was a cornerstone. She remembered now. She couldn't remember where it was at before. It had been like that of a best friend she had lost contact with, bearing her thoughts for her.

She needed that cornerstone. Before her, she saw a solid rock. Suddenly a name flowed through the recesses of her consciousness. Jesus. He was the cornerstone.

"I'm sorry. Oh God! Jesus, I'm sorry," Evelyn whimpered. She reached the phone and she dialed. When the reverend picked up on the other end of the line, her throat constricted in fear. Quentin would kill her. She envisioned the rock again. She reached for it. If only she could hang on.

Quentin's threatening words screeched in her ears drowning out all sound. Evelyn only moaned, "Jesus." The reverend heard the name rise from her lips.

"Evelyn! Yes, Evelyn! Fight!"

"Reverend Jackson tell Micah the truth. Please." Tears streamed from her eyes. The tears cast valleys along her cheeks. "The only way he can win is if he knows the truth. Please help to save my son. Don't let Quentin take his soul." Evelyn slid the phone back into the cradle. Then she blacked out.

She had done what she could.

Chapter 37

Reverend Jackson summoned Micah to the New Jersey Institute of Living. They walked in the brilliant autumn sunlight together. The day was brisk and windy. Both men walked with their collars pulled up.

The reverend had contacted Micah for an urgent meeting. He had chosen this place as the meeting ground. It was the place where Silky had grown up. Micah wondered at his choice. But he knew the reverend had been involved with the orphanage and with orphaned children for a great many years.

There was something else he wondered about too, but it could wait. The time would come.

"I've been following the murders, Micah. I wanted to talk to you about them. I do think you're on the right track, from what you've said. David Edward Stokes—Silky, as you knew him—grew up here. He was a friend of Shaughn Braswell. The two of them were thick as thieves. Never mingled outside of themselves."

Micah wondered why the name Shaughn Braswell sounded familiar to him. Then it came to him. "Wait a minute. There's a Shaughn Braswell who peddles sculptures in downtown Newark. Is he the same one?"

"One and the same. Believe me. Dangerous and dark, that one. His powers are not of this world, Micah."

Micah looked a bit surprised as a picture of a laid-back Shaughn, with impeccable manners and a long ponytail, flashed through his mind. But he didn't comment for the moment.

The reverend stopped walking. He stared past Micah almost hypnotically. Micah watched him. His feet were rooted to the spot. He didn't like the look on the reverend's face.

The reverend looked into the distant past as the brisk, sunny, autumn day faded from his view. He recalled his glimpse inside madness for Micah.

"They used to conduct rituals. Shaughn and David. They never stopped. On and on it went."

The years fell away like melting dewdrops. The reverend was face to face with the past. Micah Jordan-Wells made the journey with him.

It had happened down in the basement of the institution. The reverend stood in the dark shadows afraid. He was mesmerized by what he was witnessing. Through no will of his own, he was fixed to the spot.

A young Shaughn stood in the middle of a circle. It was made out of blazing candles. He stood on top of a flaming "X" that glowed pure red and gold flames. Yet his bare feet were not even burning.

Shaughn's eyes were transformed. They were translucent. They were hypnotic. His eyes were dark black glowing coals. They were pure emptiness shining through the night. They streamed an eerie and incandescent light.

He was dressed in a monk's outfit. The hood was pulled over his head. The tunic was roped and knotted at the waist.

The reverend watched. He didn't dare breathe.

David stared at Shaughn. He was completely under Shaughn's spell. He had no will. He had no control over his own limbs. Nor did he have any will over his own mind. He was an empty shell. Waiting to be possessed.

The reverend stifled a gasp. He fingered the cross, which hung from his neck.

Shaughn said to David, "Your soul is now in my command."

Shaughn thrust out his right fist. The "X" glowed. Shaughn shouted at David. "Do you surrender?"

David's dreamlike state never changed. "Yes."

"Good. Then I am the master of all that you are." In that instant Shaughn possessed David.

Shaughn turned his head with an air of command. A rushing wind blew through the room. The room turned upside down. A funnel of air created total chaos. Objects flew. They banged around.

Shaughn stared at David. Light streamed from his eyes. He lifted David's body from the floor. It slammed against the wall. Shaughn twirled in the circle. His arms outstretched.

His image superimposed itself on all the walls, blown up, surrounding him. Shaughn was the inheritor. He was the inheritor of a great, dark kingdom. He was the ruler of souls! He laughed. Glory and immortality were upon him.

"There is only one thing left between me and the ultimate power. I am my brother's keeper." His eyes gleamed.

He knelt in the circle. He bowed his head. The candles flickered around him. The wind in the room ceased. The room returned to normal.

Shaughn passed into a trance, whispering, "The final twinning will take place the day my brother steps foot on this property."

Shaughn lifted his head. He stared at the area where the reverend was hiding outside the door.

The reverend feared that Shaughn had spotted him. He stepped back from the peephole. He shivered in his hiding place. All was silent. He breathed a sigh of relief. Shaughn didn't know he was there. He turned to leave.

Upon turning, he came face to face with Quentin Curry. Quentin was dressed identically to Shaughn. The piercing eyes blazed at the reverend from beneath the hood. The reverend retreated backward. He tripped over some old wood lying on the floor. He could feel the waves of darkness emanating from Quentin.

The evil that Quentin generated was a tangible thing. The reverend could reach out and touch it. A cloudy haze seeped up from the ground. It cloaked the charismatic figure in front of him.

"Need I introduce myself?" Quentin said.

"No. I know all about you."

"That's good. Surely a man of the cloth understands that destiny and prophecy are entwined as one. As such, it must not be disturbed."

The reverend nodded. He could hardly believe that this man was the devil. But he knew he was. He had always thought of Quentin as a spirit. He wondered what had happened to allow him to come to earth as a man. Because just as surely as he was standing here, he knew it was him in the flesh and while he had been visiting, he had reproduced himself. The reverend closed his eyes against the stark reality of it all.

Quentin watched him. He read the reverend's thoughts.

"Yes, I have reproduced," Quentin, said. He smiled. "There can only be one power in the end of things. The night of the final twinning will declare who that will be."

Again the reverend nodded. To his horror, he discovered he was incapable of speaking. He thrust his old tree bark cross a bit in front of him since he was not able to form words.

Quentin smiled engagingly at the reverend as one smiles sometimes at an errant child. Then he threw his hands in the air, in the act of surrender. He bowed his head slightly. Then he was gone. A rushing wind swept the reverend back against the wall.

The reverend shivered from the memory of it. He opened his eyes to find Micah staring at him. For a heart stopping moment in time, a scary image flashed in front of him. He saw Quentin's eyes, and now Micah's.

The reverend frowned.

There was that feeling again. The same one he had experienced while studying Micah's photograph in the newspaper. He was slightly disturbed. He stared off into the distance. Micah tried to digest all he had just learned.

Returning his attention to Micah he saw the questions in his eyes. The reverend said, "The time has come. What do you need to know?"

"Why didn't you come forward about Silky when the women were being murdered?"

His question stung the reverend deep. He knew Micah felt betrayed. "I was under a sacred oath. There is commitment and loyalty that must be upheld."

"At the risk of the loss of life, Reverend?"

The reverend swallowed hard. "I offer no excuses, Micah. It wasn't time. I couldn't."

Micah looked closely at the reverend he'd known since childhood. "I know why Silky was here. Why was Shaughn Braswell here?"

Reverend Jackson sighed. He faced the ultimate moment of truth. As Micah had so justly pointed out, he had already been silent too long. There was also Evelyn to consider. At whatever cost, he would help to save her son.

Looking at Micah directly, he said, "His mother was afraid of him. She was afraid of his father. Of the evil they demonstrated. In her one and only act of defiance, she refused to keep Shaughn and placed him here."

"He was placed here when he was six years old. Shaughn's father threatened to kill her if she ever tried to leave. He allowed the removal of Shaughn only because it suited his needs. Shaughn's mother is a reclusive and prominent woman."

The reverend turned away. He was unable to meet Micah's eyes. Micah sensed that this was not the time to interrupt. He waited patiently.

Turning back to Micah, the reverend said, "She went to great lengths to cover her relationship with him. She had another child to protect, one who wasn't like Shaughn. One who was caring and loving. He's different in every way."

"Nevertheless, I believe Shaughn found out who she is. He went on a murdering rampage. He used Silky. He's leaving his mark for her. Waiting for her to recognize it. He's leaving his mark for the world to see. I can't prove anything, of course. It's just my own feeling. But I also believe her life is in great danger."

"Who is Shaughn Braswell's mother?"

The reverend's eyes glittered. He didn't immediately answer. He placed both hands on Micah's shoulders. "Understand, Micah, that I am bound by the laws of man since I am part of the orphanage to keep that information confidential. But I am also bound by the higher law of God to release the truth."

It really wasn't a decision. He had no choice. But he had felt the need to say that, to make it clear. Besides, Evelyn had finally stepped out. And for that she would be rewarded. Her son would be given what he needed to fight back.

"Shaughn's mother is . . . Evelyn Braswell Jordan-Wells." The name dropped like a rock in the middle of a lake, causing the smooth surface to ripple from the shock of it.

"She is the famed novelist also known as Blaine Upshaw. Micah, Shaughn Braswell is your brother."

A startled, shocked gasp of air exited Micah's lungs. A sharp stab of pain shot through his gut. He leaned over from the force of it. His eyes reflected shocked disbelief.

Micah pulled the collar of his coat around his neck. His head pounded. Shadowy images floated before his eyes. Images he had suppressed in the deep recesses of his memory. The reverend's words had unlocked the door. The memories tumbled forward in full force.

There was a six-year-old boy looking out the window. His nose was pressed against the filmy glass. It was made steamy from his breath. He wiped the window with his small hand so he could see.

Another little boy was crying. It was sad and tragic. A man was taking him from the house against his will. The boy was fighting the man. He was struggling. He tried to run back to the house. He yelled out, "Mommy! Mommy!"

The boy broke the grip. He ran. He tried to reach his mother. But the man caught him. The man.

Who was that man?

Micah peered closer. The reverend's face swam before his eyes in vivid clarity.

It had been long buried. Forgotten, until now. Micah remembered. With that memory came pain, shock and outrage.

He looked into the reverend's eyes. The evidence of the truth stared back at him. The small things were adding up for him. Tallying up in fact with the speed of light. Micah dared not to check the total.

"There is more, Micah."

"How the hell can there be more? Don't you think that's enough?"

Reverend Erwin Jackson nodded sadly. But he had to go on if he were to protect Micah. He landed the last and final blow with a volume of not much more than a whisper, "Micah, you and Shaughn Braswell are identical twins. Mirror images. Shaughn's looks are altered because looking at him, for you, would be like looking in the mirror. Genetically speaking, you have the same voice and the same mannerisms. There is absolutely no way to tell the two of you apart . . ."

Micah closed his eyes against the harshness of the day. He stood rigidly in place as the pieces of the puzzle slowly dropped into their designated spots. Of all the scenarios he had envisioned, this was not one of them.

The deceit had been so complete he'd wondered if maybe he *had* committed the murders. Maybe he had blacked out and killed them. All along, the secrets of his past had been haunting him.

Hatred, vile and venomous, rose up from his belly. He asked the final question. One more thing that was still niggling at him, "Who is our father?"

"Your father and Shaughn's father is Quentin Curry." The reverend described him. Micah flashed back to the image of Quentin in his bedroom. He heard Quentin's words, "It doesn't matter who I am. All that matters is who you are. You're demon spawned."

"Only fate played a cruel trick on him, Micah," the reverend said, "when it came to you."

Micah didn't want to hear any more. He walked away.

"Micah! There's more. You can't win if you don't know it all." The reverend ran to catch up to him.

Micah glided to a halt. His eyes beamed a strange, angry glow, seizing the reverend in its grip.

"Quentin Curry has no past or present, Micah. No birth records exist, no driver's license, no social security number, and no fingerprints. Nothing. Years ago, your mother and I tried. She was so afraid of him she developed agoraphobia. That's why she hasn't left the house since your birth. When trying to get rid of him didn't work, she stopped trying. His power was stronger than hers.

"That and the fact that he told her he would kill you if she ever left. He told her he would kill the both of you. You are the only good thing that has ever happened to Evelyn."

The reverend grabbed Micah by the shoulders. He gave him a penetrating look, willing him, praying for him to understand. For years he hadn't gotten through to Evelyn, but he would not let Micah be lost too.

He hadn't gotten through to Evelyn but something had.

He knew Evelyn had put her life in jeopardy by calling him. She had risked her life to save Micah's life. She had fought for him to know the truth.

He could impart the knowledge that would help Micah win. He was not letting him leave without it.

"Micah, what I'm trying to say is you can't stop Quentin, or the demon he spawned, with the laws you work with. You also can't believe you're one of them, because you are not. You're not like them.

You can't arrest and convict Quentin Curry, because for all points and purposes he doesn't exist. Do you understand what I'm saying to you?"

Finally Micah did.

He understood it all. It was an age-old play off. Only he was not the inheritor of the bad seed. It was a mind game, designed to make him think he was something he was not. It was a game of possession. They had tried to destroy his sanity. If he had truly been like them there would have been no need to convince him. No need for the games. Somewhere deceit still lurked. And Micah knew without a doubt it was generating from Quentin Curry.

Micah squinted at the sun. It brightened and moved a little closer to the earth. It bathed him in a simple truth that resounded throughout his entire being. He had been taught at the reverend's knee. Given the weapons a long time ago. He felt a presence. He turned.

Behind him was the old man Isaac who had approached him on the street. "God is good, God is great," he said. Then he took off his derby. He bowed once again before Micah. And this time he did something different. He reached into his collar, and thrust forth the tree bark cross. Micah reached in his collar, thrusting forth an identical one. Old Isaac nodded. Then he disappeared. The other two crosses belonged to the reverend.

Micah drew strength. It was a mighty strength. It came from the light. He realized he had been given a gift. What he had thought was a curse was a blessing, a gift.

Special gifts were there for a reason. He must learn how to use it. The revelation opened to him just as petals on a flower open on a spring day.

He returned his gaze to the reverend, "Yes, Reverend. I do understand."

The reverend felt a shift. As though the very earth had tilted. He was satisfied with what he saw reflected in Micah's eyes. That was what had been disturbing him. In Micah's eyes was great power. But it was not a power born of evil. Bless God!

"Go with God, Micah. Go with God."

Micah's eyes shone brightly with unshed tears. He nodded at the reverend respectfully, then turned and walked away.

Chapter 38

Micah Jordan-Wells had stepped foot on the grounds of the New Jersey Institute of Living. With that single step he had set off a course of events destined to take place.

The Victorian house stood ready. It was built for the very events that would take place that night.

Eons ago, Quentin had chosen carefully. He had laid the groundwork. All of it had been skillfully planned. Tonight's twinning between Shaughn and Micah would give him everything he needed.

Today, Micah Jordan-Wells had fulfilled a prophecy that had been long ago written, destined, and etched into history. War had been declared.

Quentin smoked a cigarette. He stared at Evelyn's prized and precious Victorian. He pulled on the cigarette. He watched the stillness of the house. His mark had been put on it long ago.

He smiled as he recalled the moment he had arrived at the supreme plan. He had created the perfect womb. By implanting his seed in Evelyn's womb, he had assured himself of continuous longevity in the form of a man. Instead of constantly recruiting new spirits, he had gained the power of reproduction.

The most awesome thing about it was that instead of merely inhabiting different bodies, he had gained the opportunity to live in them, again and again, while still possessing the powers of the spirit.

Once the twinning took place and the two powers merged into one, he would gain the ultimate status. The twinning would create a power structure the likes of which mankind had never experienced here on earth.

He would be ruler of another great kingdom, without anyone being the wiser. In Shaughn, he would have the ability to fight the war on earth when the time came. Ultimately, he would rule on earth once the chosen ones had been defeated.

He would be the ruler of earth. He took another drag from the cigarette. He laughed at the simplicity of man's mind.

He knew that most men who believed at all thought the ultimate war would be fought in heaven. They thought only certain prophecies would be fulfilled on earth. They had never imagined that earth would become a domain, and whoever ruled, would rule the world.

Right now there was a split. Between his people and those of Christ. But soon he would rule it all, because as he destroyed their faith, he destroyed their weapons. If they didn't believe, they wouldn't obtain salvation. If they didn't have salvation, they wouldn't be under the protection of Jesus Christ.

Oh, what a wonderful world it was. He couldn't wait. Once the twinning took place, it wouldn't take long for him to scare the belief right out of most of them. All that would be left would be him. He was killing off the marked ones before they could produce a warrior, who would find favor with God to defeat him.

He stubbed out the cigarette. He was disturbed as he thought about the curve ball he had been thrown. That curve ball was Micah Jordan-Wells.

When Evelyn had produced twins instead of one son, it had thrown him for a loop. At first he was deliriously happy. He thought he had been granted a great gift beyond what he had contemplated in the form of not one but two sons.

It hadn't taken him long to realize, however, that he was wrong. He observed things in Micah not to his liking. Micah was different from Shaughn.

Upon inspecting Micah's DNA, he realized Micah was of a different structure, not born of him but of a different man and yet he had inhabited the same womb as Shaughn and emerged with identical traits.

Upon discovering this information, Quentin had been incensed when he learned he had also been rendered powerless to do anything about this development. Micah Jordan-Wells had become off limits to his powers. Although, not off limits to his tricks.

That was why he had allowed Evelyn to place Shaughn in an institution. He knew he would have to work twice as hard to ready Shaughn for the upcoming battle.

The ultimate power had been divided between them. Only through twinning could the power be contained in one body. He intended to make sure that body belonged to Shaughn.

It had been the highest level of treachery. But he would prevail. He was well prepared.

Evelyn had never known about the deceit that had taken place in her womb. As Quentin watched Micah grow, the deceit had become more and more apparent.

Micah's father had been a stranger in the night. Quentin shook his head at the audacity of Evelyn. To think she pulled this off without his knowledge. She hadn't.

However, she had unknowingly accomplished, in her quest for purification from him, the superceding of his sperm. Once the egg divided in her womb. Micah had been fathered by sperm other than his.

Micah Jordan-Wells was a common man's son.

Evelyn possessed a double edge that he hadn't counted on originally. The man was a mere beggar who had shown up at her door for a handout, a one-night stand that altered the course of history.

Quentin shook his fist in a rage at the remembrance of it. But now he would prevail. All he had to do was to wrest the other half of the power from Micah Jordan-Wells. Then he could be made whole.

Chapter 39

Evelyn was in her kitchen. She felt better than she had in a long time. She had awakened from her blackout thinking she would be dead and in hell. However, she was still here. So, she had decided to cook.

Her kitchen was the ultimate of any cook's dream. Copper and stainless steel pans hung from the rafters. The smell of fresh vegetables permeated the kitchen with a warm aroma from the soup Evelyn was cooking.

She was baking warm fresh bread as well as homemade cookies. Cooking sometimes provided therapy for her soul. She enjoyed baking from scratch.

There were four range tops and three ovens as well as a modernized counter, which sat in the middle of the kitchen. A stone hearth fireplace was situated in the corner.

In front of the fireplace was a couch piled high with downy soft pillows that faced a three-hundred-year-old chintz-covered table. The table was littered with magazines of every sort.

The kitchen was the only room in the house that had been modernized. Although Evelyn didn't entertain, she was a great fan of atmosphere. Plants hung around the kitchen, each in their own little ornate holders. And Evelyn loved to cook.

In her kitchen, Evelyn pretended many times that her life was normal. Everything looked and smelled normal, just like any other ordinary family kitchen. Out of her longing, she had created a mirage, nothing more nor less.

It was simply her instinct for survival. For her, it was retribution in the form of a mere room and some cooking utensils.

The futility of her life washed over her in great waves as she stirred the soup. A teardrop fell in the broth. A memory she had long ago tucked in the back of her mind rose up in front of her. About the night Quentin took her to implant his seed.

That same night a beggar had showed up at her door. She had taken him into her bed. He had been her denial against an insanity she couldn't believe. Against an event her mind refused to accept. A way to wash herself clean of the vileness that was Quentin Curry.

It wasn't plausible. She couldn't believe she had done such a thing. The raw fear of it was written inside her soul. Yet for a moment in time, yes, just one moment in time, a man who was homeless and begging had restored normalcy to her life and some peace to her soul in the process.

She had never seen or heard from him again. He had passed like a ship in the night. Then he was gone. Like a dream you awake from, unsure that you even really had it.

To make matters worse, Quentin had achieved what he wanted. He had implanted his vile seed in her, and she became pregnant. She had tried to talk to the reverend. She tried to explain why she couldn't have the baby but he had told her she couldn't abort. He said, "God had a way of working things out, in His time and in His way."

She stirred the pot more vigorously as the memories flooded the forefront of her mind, swamping her with emotion. Over thirty years had passed. She was still waiting for things to work out.

Every night she had prayed to be released. She had prayed to let it pass her by. She prayed for answers on how something like this could have happened. All she had received in return was silence, a deafening silence. And now Quentin was in full form.

He was stamping out lives and leaving his mark and, through her womb, he had gained a life force through which he would gain eternal life on earth.

"My Lord." She had been uttering that phrase for years. Evelyn sipped from her cup of coffee.

She looked up as she heard the front door in the foyer creak open. Micah. She went to the living room. Shaughn was standing there.

She smiled, glad to see him. "Micah."

Upon her arrival, Shaughn's alter excitedly pushed to the forefront and came out to greet Evelyn. "Hi, Mommy. It's me. You remember me, Vaughn."

Shaughn grabbed Vaughn. He pushed him back to the deep dark place. As Evelyn watched, a strange war took place in Shaughn's body.

"Yeah, Evelyn," Shaughn, who was back in control, said viciously. "You remember me, right?"

A gripping shock poured through Evelyn's body like ice water running through her veins. She took a step back from Shaughn. "Shaughn? No," she mumbled.

Shaughn took a step forward. "Oh yeah, Mommy dearest," he sneered.

Evelyn shut her eyes. She had known this day would come. It was unavoidable. The reverend had warned her. She had not wanted to believe him.

The day had arrived with what now seemed like the speed of a roller coaster. Here he was in the flesh. Standing before her very eyes. Her head ached as though she had been struck by a two-by-four. Her past stared at her hauntingly.

She sighed deeply, taking in his full appearance before asking, "Why are you dressed like that? You're not Micah. Why are you trying to be Micah?"

Evelyn had never, not even when they were small boys and she still had custody of Shaughn, ever tried to dress them identically.

In fact she had done everything in her power to make them different. The one thing she had realized from the beginning was that Micah *was* different. They looked identical. But on close inspection she could tell them apart. Shaughn's eyes were simply a dark black void, nothing else.

She wondered why he had called himself Vaughn. She had been startled as she watched two distinct personalities greet her in the same body. In a flash, everything about the physicality of the body had changed.

Shaughn watched her careful evaluation. He was a patient man.

He had waited for a long time. There was no need to rush things. Shaughn mimicked her, "You're not Micah." He laughed. "No, I'm not Micah, and Micah won't be Micah for very much longer." Shaughn looked smug. He relished the very idea of no more Micah.

Vaughn was choking in the dark place. He couldn't handle being there. He could hear Evelyn's voice. Hers was a voice he had been craving to hear for a very long time. He wanted her to hold him.

Maybe she had his favorite raspberry sherbet and some books he could color in. He smelled something good coming from the kitchen. He couldn't stay in the dark place. He wanted his mommy. He wanted her to hold him, to play with him.

Vaughn concentrated very hard.

He focused on Shaughn's hands. They were around his neck trying to keep him at bay. If he focused hard enough he could break the grip. He just had to want to, like when he wanted to color. Focus, focus—slowly Shaughn's hands loosened, and at the first opening, Vaughn broke through to the surface.

Shaughn's body, his stance, and his demeanor changed to that of a six-year-old boy and Vaughn reached out to touch her. Tears welled up in his eyes. "Mommy."

Something inside Evelyn snapped as she realized what had happened. She recognized Vaughn. He was Shaughn, when Shaughn was six years old, the day she gave him away.

The knowledge that his personality must have split in two on his separation from her broke her down. A physical pain sliced through her chest. Her eyes glittered with bright, shining tears like jewels in a showcase.

Her chest felt as though someone had physically severed it with a knife. "Oh, God, Shaughn. Oh, God." For a moment in time, she was simply a mother who had lost a child. She had lost a child to a horrible and wretched evil.

Vaughn reached out and she took him in her arms. She held him tightly. Vaughn asked, "Do you have any raspberry sherbet? I like raspberry sherbet." She remembered that as a boy, it had been Shaughn's favorite. She took his hand and led him to the kitchen.

Vaughn sat at the center counter like a typical six-year-old while Evelyn rummaged in the freezer for the sherbet. Actually, it was one of her favorites as well. She found the sherbet and scooped it into a bowl for Vaughn.

She placed the dish in front of him. She sipped her coffee while watching him dig in gleefully. Between mouthfuls he said, "Do you have any coloring books? I like to color."

Evelyn watched him for a moment. "No, but I do have some color markers and paper. Would you like to sketch?" Vaughn nodded vigorously.

Evelyn retrieved the items. She set them in front of Vaughn on the counter. She took a seat across the counter island from him.

Vaughn drew stick figures on the paper. He hummed a little tune to himself. He swung his legs to the beat. He looked up at her and giggled. He was so happy just being with her. This was where he had belonged all along.

Guilt splashed all over Evelyn reminding her of her abandonment of him. "I've always loved you, Shaughn." To an extent it was true. Even though his conception was under cruel and unusual circumstances.

As she watched the little boy, she was caught up in the moment. She forgot about the circumstances. Vaughn piped up, "I love you too, Mommy." He grinned in her direction.

He couldn't remember when he had been so content. This was nice. "Can I have some soup, too?" Evelyn smiled her answer.

Inside the dark place Shaughn had had enough. He was ripping. He couldn't believe this witch had the nerve to say she loved him. She had tossed him away like so much garbage without a backward glance. For that she would pay.

Dark rage assaulted Shaughn. It rippled through his entire body. He snatched Vaughn back so hard that Vaughn's neck snapped in the process. Vaughn didn't have a chance to mutter even the slightest protest.

Before Vaughn realized it, he was back in the dark place with no sherbet, no sketching paper and no soup. Distraught, Vaughn cried. He whined. He screamed. But he couldn't break Shaughn's iron grip this time. He'd have to wait for a soft spot to break through again. Shaughn didn't have soft spots all that often.

Vaughn's screaming was getting on Shaughn's nerves. "Shut up, you little punk. I'm warning you, Vaughn," he told him. "Shut up!"

Shaughn turned his attention to Evelyn. Pure venom dripped from his eyes. Without touching her, Shaughn's hatred reached out and virtually shook Evelyn like a rag doll.

He swept his arm across the counter knocking the remaining sherbet, along with the markers and sketching paper, to the floor.

Evelyn screamed.

She jumped up from her chair. In the space of a second, her idyllic lapse in memory was snatched away. She ran down the hall and into the solarium, locking the door behind her.

A flash of the past rolled before her eyes. She had done this before with Quentin. Oh God! The past was about to repeat itself.

Trembling, she listened. She didn't hear anything. She put her back to the door. Evelyn breathed in great gulps of air, trying to talk herself down, but it wasn't working. She was seized with the feeling to look up at the glass roof, but she didn't want to.

Unable to resist the force of the feeling, she looked up. The past stared straight at her. Shaughn Braswell lay splayed on the glass roof. He made eye-to-eye contact with Evelyn, touching her very soul.

In a shower of glass, Shaughn crashed through to land in front of Evelyn. He was lithe and agile on his feet. Shaughn was in her realm. The force of his gaze backed her away.

"Hello, Mother. Are you trying to get away from me?" Shaughn's naked hatred of Evelyn raged across his face. He looked at her, remembering a long-ago ritual with his father. With startling clarity he recalled his initiation into power and manhood.

Shaughn had been twelve years old at the time. He stood before Quentin Curry in a circle of candles. Inside the circle was an "X" molten into the floor.

"Shaughn," Quentin said.

Shaughn held out his right hand balled into a fist. Quentin branded an "X" directly into the skin. Quentin watched intently as Shaughn bore the pain of the searing heat. Shaughn knew he must not cry out.

Shaughn's face twitched in agony. His whole body quivered as a force moved inside him.

Quentin stared hypnotically into Shaughn's eyes. "You now bear the mark of the 'X.' You are Criss Cross. My namesake. The name itself has great power. When the time comes, you will twin with your brother from whom you've been separated. You will be the victor in the twinning and emerge with all the power.

"Upon my death in this body, the greatest power on earth will pass to you. You will then defeat the ones with the mark of the six in the time of war. In order to be whole you must possess the other half of the power, which your brother, Micah Jordan-Wells, holds. You, Shaughn, are the chosen one. You are Criss Cross. Criss Cross embodies the mightiest power on earth. I am he. But now you will be. To you I pass the torch."

Quentin doused the candles. He looked ferociously at the "X" under Shaughn's feet. It became a blaze of burning fire, yet the fire did not burn Shaughn's bare feet. Shaughn watched Quentin with adoration. He bowed deeply before him, worshipping him.

Quentin was pleased with how Shaughn had come through this important round. He then explained to him the mind-numbing piece, the part he must always remember.

"Everything must follow the pattern of the 'X.' Never deviate. It is sacred. Your mother broke the tie that binds when she gave you away. She banished you. Cut you out. But the 'X' ensures you can never ever be severed. It is binding. I have redeemed you."

What Quentin hadn't told Shaughn was one *very* important fact. Quentin would have to take the body that Shaughn was occupying when the time came. In the process, Shaughn would die, leaving Quentin the only victor.

He had managed to be able to reproduce himself in man's world, but what he couldn't overcome was the death of the body. Man's body aged, man's body became ill and eventually a man's body died. Quentin would forever need a new body in order to survive on earth. Once Quentin took possession of Shaughn's body, Shaughn would be extinguished forever.

It was the ultimate in deception, but that was who he was. He had been deceiving man since the beginning of time.

Shaughn nodded at Quentin's orders. He smiled at the thought of the power that would one day be his.

As Evelyn watched Shaughn's eyes cleared. He returned his attention to her. Evelyn hyperventilated. She gasped out, "No!"

Shaughn arrogantly stepped forward in a smooth stroke reminiscent of Micah.

Evelyn, recognizing the move, clutched her chest. The pain was so sharp she thought she was going to have a heart attack. Yes, a heart attack would be good, preferable even.

She couldn't live through this hell anymore. Suddenly she was repulsed by the fact that Shaughn could take on Micah's qualities.

Her skin crawled as the realization of the murders, the atrocities he must have committed, and the terror he must have inflicted on others, as well as the beast that he must've become, fell like tiny bits of micro-information in her mind.

She was horrified at the senseless evil.

Shaughn reached into her mind and probed her thoughts. He felt her repulsion. She shook her head and he smiled. "Evelyn Braswell Jordan-Wells. Yes, I can be Micah when I want to. Does that bother you? Do you think he's too pure to get his hands dirty as I have?"

Evelyn tried to back up but there was nowhere to go.

"You're a tiebreaker," Shaughn told her. "So many dead women. There were six in all. How many times do I have to kill you?"

Shaughn's breathing escalated. "Why didn't you just stay dead?!"

Evelyn's eyes widened.

"Silky was a puppet," Shaughn said, relishing the facts of his story, "I was the one who sculpted and took the time to set up your portrait. You are a portrait you know, nothing more, all pretty on the outside and nothing inside."

Shaughn laughed as he remembered. "Silky wouldn't know art if it slapped him in the face. That was one body I was glad to get out of. The man was a simpering, whining fool. All that drama, still pining for his mama."

Evelyn's hands flew to her mouth. Shaughn continued to look at her intently. "You're also a whore, you know." Evelyn gasped, as Shaughn crawled down into the gutter of the English language. "How could I come from the womb of a whore? You're just like them. Only you're worse because you slept with the enemy."

"Stop it!" Evelyn screamed at him. "Stop it!"

Vaughn was unable to bear Evelyn's cries of anguish. When Shaughn let his mind drift for a moment, Vaughn scurried for the front position. He stumbled out and fell at Evelyn's feet.

"Hold me, Mommy!" Vaughn reached up to her as she backed away, inching her way toward the door, but Shaughn shoved Vaughn out of the way and climbed to his feet.

The air in the room was possessed with a dark presence. It rippled with force. Contaminated rage streaked across Shaughn's face. He reached out a hand. He touched her hair. He smoothed his hand across her dark thick locks peppered with gray.

Evelyn cringed. He went on stroking. Shaughn's voice turned to a soft whisper, "Hold me, Mommy."

Evelyn's arms were frozen in place. Shaughn's voice took on a dreamy quality. "You are such a perfect beauty. Just like a mother should be. I'm your son. I'm your first born by two minutes. You didn't know I knew that, did you? Hold me."

Evelyn stared up at him. Stark fear sprayed from her eyes. It carved itself across her features. Her face turned into a hideous mask.

Shaughn tightened his hand on her hair. He yanked her head so hard, Evelyn's neck snapped from the sheer force of it. A bolt of pain shot through her. He screamed in her face, his rage boiling to the surface, "I said hold me! Pretend I'm your precious Micah! Put your arms around me and say you love me! Do it!

Evelyn's arms flew around his neck. Shaughn leaned in her face and yelled, "Say it!"

Evelyn could feel his hot breath in her face. His eyes were void. There was nothing there. A deep dark pit of nothingness beheld her.

She forced the bile back down into her belly, which rose in her throat. She croaked out, "I . . . I . . . I . . . I . . . love you."

"You're a liar! You're also a walking dead woman!"

Vaughn was weeping. He tried to get air. He found a surge of strength. The most he had ever had and, for a second in time, he shoved Shaughn into the deep dark place and yelled out, "No! Don't kill her! No, Shaughn! I don't want her to die!"

He had just found his mother. She couldn't die. Shaughn couldn't kill her. He wouldn't let him. What was wrong with him? Vaughn struggled to keep Shaughn in the dark place so he could have control of the body, "No, Shaughn!" he shouted.

Evelyn watched. Her heart reached out to Vaughn, but he was no match for Shaughn. If she could figure out a way to keep Vaughn out, she might have a chance, but Shaughn's hatred of her was so powerful that Vaughn didn't stand a chance and she knew it.

Before Evelyn could think of a thing to do or say, Shaughn was back. He now shoved Vaughn down into the third level of darkness. Vaughn was really scared. He had never been down this deep. He was crying.

"Shut up!" Shaughn told him. "I'm sick of your whining."

Shaughn was straight bugging out now. In front of Evelyn's startled eyes, Shaughn and Vaughn flipped back and forth. Vaughn didn't want to be at this level. It was too dark. He was lonely, afraid.

With another powerful surge of strength he didn't know he possessed, Vaughn floated to the surface. Shaughn was flipping back and forth between his alter and himself.

Getting sick of the game of tug of war he and Vaughn were engaged in, Shaughn glanced in the mirror. With a withering glance at Vaughn he was back in control. This time when he pushed Vaughn into the third level, he told him, "I don't need you anymore. Be gone."

An electric pop shook the body. It killed the electricity in the room; such was the power of it.

Vaughn found himself falling, falling into the deep dark space, one level and then two levels. The levels kept coming and coming until he didn't know how many he had passed. He struggled, but all of his might had somehow been sapped from him. The abyss was just up ahead. He could see it waiting to catch him.

Vaughn reached the circle of darkness. He was sucked in by a whirlwind. His voice was extinguished and finally silenced on the way down into the whirling pool of black. Vaughn's last words were. "I love you, Mommy. I love you."

And then he was gone.

The lights dimmed and then came back on. Shaughn was back in control, full control. His alter had been silenced forever. He would never hear Vaughn's whining voice again. He didn't need him nor did he want him anymore.

Having witnessed Vaughn's death, Evelyn crumbled. She knew the only chance Shaughn might have had for redemption was now dead and gone—and buried with him was her only hope for survival.

Evelyn shook so hard her teeth rattled. Shaughn was not moved. "Like I said, you are a walking dead woman. The payment is due, Evelyn. I want you to die. You didn't want me and now I don't want you."

Shaughn paced the solarium. His spirit was restless. He needed to kill her. He would once he'd had his say.

"How does it feel?" He paused in his pacing, rethinking his plan. "You know what, Evelyn. I've decided that first your precious baby goes. You know him. Micah Jordan-Wells. After you stare into his eyes dulled by death, then and only then will it be your turn to die. First you suffer. Then you die."

Evelyn screamed. She reached for Shaughn's throat, choking him. She wanted to choke the blackness right out of him. He pushed her viciously away. Then backhanded her with the force of ten men.

Evelyn struck her head on the edge of the fountain. She blacked out. Blood trickled from her forehead and the side of her mouth. Shaughn laughed. He spat on her. She was a selfish witch if he'd ever seen one. "You're garbage!" he told the figure on the floor.

Shaughn headed into the kitchen for a bowl of soup. He sniffed the air, the aroma smelled delicious. After he ate, he would get ready to come face to face with Micah.

"Micah Jordan Wells. Yeah," he said, "It's been a long time coming, Micah. Now it's time for the prophecy to be fulfilled. I'll tell you what. You can call me Criss Cross."

Shaughn was jubilant with power.

He loved the way the name Criss Cross rolled off his tongue. More than that, he loved what it meant. It was the highest pinnacle of power. He was the inheritor of Quentin Curry, the man who never slept. The man, who simply put, was power.

Yeah. It was time to get it on. It was time for him to take his place in history.

After all he *was* Criss Cross . . .

Chapter 40

Micah recklessly screeched to a halt in front of Evelyn's house. A quiet rain fell washing the city of Newark in its wetness. Micah leaped from the car. He ran up to the house, inserting his key in the lock.

He stepped inside the foyer and came face to face with Shaughn. Shaughn watched him sardonically. He sized him up. The two locked eyes. The battle was already raging in their souls.

Micah was stunned at the identical resemblance. Here was the brother he never knew. Once again Shaughn had altered his appearance. The one he would have to take down. He was a celebrated detective, risking his life to right the wrongs of society.

His brother was a sadistic serial killer of demonic proportions. Ironically, he had been born of the same woman as Micah. And she had been forced to abandon one of her children, most notably because he was demon spawn. The irony of this was not lost on him.

Quentin Curry had taken her life away. Micah Jordan-Wells would destroy him for that single act. He had forced darkness into her womb. Now its manifestation stood looking at him.

Quentin Curry had taken away her weapons through fear, intimidation. He had dominated her. But ultimately he had beaten her down by ripping the very foundation from underneath her feet. He had taken away her most powerful weapon. That had been her faith in God.

A dark veil fell over Micah's face. He witnessed death, the death of one life and the resurrection of another. Now it would be a different story. He had the power to rewrite the ending, and rewrite it he would.

First, he would dispense of Quentin's seed. Then he would dispense with Quentin.

Micah stared into the mirror image before him. The eyes were empty. They reflected darkness. The recesses were nothing more than a pit. Fury laid its hand on him. Shaughn had killed numerous women and kids for what he considered sport.

Micah was the first to speak. When he did, his voice was laced with a tone that even he didn't recognize. "So it's you," he said.

"In the flesh. Sorry Silky couldn't be here. Whoosh! Up in flames. He's gone. It really was him, you know. I left after I killed the women. Dearly departed."

Micah's eyes turned to slits. "Really. I thought that was you jumping up on the counsel table saying you were wrath."

Shaughn laughed. "I put in the occasional appearance. I told you I'd be back to eat your young. I'm back."

A glow peeked out from the depths of Shaughn's eyes. He stared at the door. It slammed shut.

Micah didn't flinch or make the slightest move.

"What is the tie that binds, Micah?"

"A mother, Shaughn. Isn't that the answer you were searching for all along? The tie that you never had."

"Very good, Micah Jordan-Wells," Shaughn drew Micah's name out, nastily, every single syllable tinged with the icicles of his hatred for Micah. "You go to the head of the class."

"Where's my mother, Shaughn?"

Micah didn't like the eerie silence of the house. He knew he would kill Shaughn without hesitation if anything had happened to Evelyn. It wasn't even a question of if. More like how soon. Shaughn was a reptile. He made Micah's skin crawl.

Instead of answering Micah's question, Shaughn said to him, "You're a rude boy, Micah."

A loud crash sounded behind Micah. Micah turned instinctively at the sound. Shaughn stepped up behind him. He hit Micah in the base of his skull with an antique paperweight that was sitting on a bookshelf, knocking him out cold.

Chapter 41

Wolfgang paced his office. Beads of sweat popped out on his forehead. He looked at the telephone for the hundredth time and still it didn't ring.

He walked over to look out the window. A heavy rain drenched Newark. He could hear the drops as they pelted against the windows. He pressed his face against the pane of glass. He watched the rain as it fell in sheets across the city.

Pure madness had gripped his department. What an arcane idea. The twinning of a cop and a serial killer, in the spirit, to gain power over some supposed war on earth. He had now heard it all.

Regardless of what he felt the killer was very real. His victims were real. He had to be stopped. The mind games of this maniac had cost them a great deal. He knew they had never been up against a killer of this particular magnitude. It could not be dismissed. It was what it was. What it was, like it or not, was real.

Even through the documented annals of crime, where evil had shown its face in many different ways this killer was of a distinctive rank. To underestimate him would be fatal.

Wolfgang walked over to his chair. He didn't know where Micah was. He had more access to Micah's life than any other human being on the earth. But he didn't know where he was.

Micah's life was in serious danger. The killer had set him up as a murder suspect, had lived his life, slept with his woman, and had put everything Micah trusted in jeopardy. In the process he had nearly destroyed his soul. It was a clever setup to say the least.

"If anyone can take him head-on, Micah can," Wolfgang spoke the words out loud. They sounded more reassuring as he listened to the sound of his own voice.

Someone knocked. Before he could say "come in," the door opened. Nugent rushed into the office. "I can't locate Micah anywhere. Where the hell is he?" Wolfgang said.

"I think I might know. I just came from having a talk with Reverend Erwin Jackson at the New Jersey Institute of Living where Silky was raised."

"And?"

Nugent pulled out a file. He laid it on the desk. Wolfgang reached for it. Nugent placed his hand on top of it.

"Before you open this I want you to know that this file belongs to one of the sons of Evelyn Braswell Jordan-Wells. The one she gave away when he was six years old."

Wolfgang stared at the file as though it had suddenly come alive. Nugent opened the file. He removed two headshots. The face of Micah Jordan-Wells was in each picture.

Nugent picked up the picture on his right. Each one was marked on the back. "This picture came from our police files. Micah Jordan-Wells."

Nugent picked up the other picture. "This picture came from the New Jersey Institute of Living. Shaughn Braswell."

Wolfgang shook his head. "What in the hell?"

"Shaughn Braswell is Micah Jordan-Wells's brother. They're identical twins. You're looking at Criss Cross."

"Incredible," Wolfgang mumbled.

"Justin was right, Wolfgang. Twinning. Shaughn believes Micah is holding the other half of the power he needs. He plans to take the power by twinning with him. The common thread is that they're brothers."

"Spiritual theft. It's a merger of the spirits just like Justin said. The reverend believes tonight is the night of the final twinning. It's a prophecy that's been planned for some time. Micah is the other half of that prophecy. Criss Cross must have Micah's half to gain the ultimate power."

Wolfgang was still looking at the pictures. "I'll be damned. You can't tell one from the other."

"That's how he was able to impersonate Micah. If he walked in here right now, neither of us would know the difference. According to the reverend his speech pattern and mannerisms are the same as Micah's."

Nugent looked out the window at the falling sheets of rain pounding the city of Newark.

"As crazy as it sounds it looks as though Shaughn was somehow in possession of Silky's body. He took complete control of him. He committed the murders of the women in Silky's body. Silky was no more than a puppet. Shaughn killed the boys on his own. He's acting out because Evelyn gave him away. Hell, he killed her six times that we know of.

"He wants to extinguish Micah. Silky told Micah in court that he didn't even know who he was. It was true. He was warning Micah. Micah is part of some weird inheritance. And he's in Criss Cross's way. For all points and purposes, it is a deadly place to be."

Nugent turned his attention from the window. "Shaughn needs the power he perceives to be Micah's. In order to gain it, he has to kill him. Tonight is the final chapter. We'd better go."

"Where?"

"Where else? We're going where it all started. Evelyn Braswell Jordan-Wells's manor. I'll explain on the way. That's where Micah is. Let's go."

Chapter 42

Precognition. Micah awoke from the blow to his neck to discover he was living his bout of precognition, live and in Technicolor in the basement of Evelyn's house.

It was dark. Pitch-black dark. Hot mist rose from the ground around Micah's feet. He struggled to free his hands and feet from the roped wired bounds. The muscles in his biceps tensed. They coiled. Micah was wired tight to a chair.

It was intensely hot in the room. The temperature soared beyond anything normal. Sweat dripped, poured into his eyes skewing his vision. He tasted the salt of it in his mouth.

His jerking around caused the wires to slice through his flesh. Red spots of blood oozed from his wrists and ankles. Then there was a sound like the roar of a rushing wind. An ear-shattering explosion burst forth. His ears popped.

Micah sat very still. He listened. He tried to identify the direction of the sound.

Red-orange light burst forth through the darkness. A flaming ball of fire rushed him. With the speed of light it was on him. He howled. A mix of denial, defiance and terror discharged from his throat.

Someone laughed. Mocked him. He heard a deep baritone voice. It held no life. It held no feeling. It echoed up to him from a deep pit. "Micah! Micah!" It drew him in, sucking him down into its tunnel. A mere instant before he would have been engulfed in flames.

A flaming "X" shone through the darkness. Molten heat seared it into the cement floor. The "X" slowly ascended. Then it branded itself over Micah's body merging with him. Gut-wrenching sounds of pure agony gushed from Micah's lips. Vomit poured forth through his parched lips.

He scooted his chair backward to resist the merger. He twisted. He turned trying to gain some distance from the frightening mark. It was all over him. He shuddered. Stark fear drenched his body. The smell of his own musk reached his nostrils.

Micah's dehydrated body jerked spastically. Sweat-dripping terror of the darkest kind drenched his body. His mind whirled in confusion.

Micah lifted his head. He found himself looking into the depths of hell. Shaughn watched him in idyllic amusement.

This time he had not awakened from the recurring dream. He was awake. The nightmare waited to devour him, ready to mark its place. To close a chapter in history that must take place at all costs.

"You have something that's mine, Micah."

"I don't have a damn thing that belongs to you."

"Oh, but you do. And you know it."

Micah stared at him.

"The prophecy will be fulfilled, just as our father declared. We will become one soul. No more separate entities. Tonight we twin. And I will control the earth's greatest power. When the time comes, I and my seed will be ready to war." Shaughn relayed the information as though Micah should have no problem understanding this.

Micah looked at Shaughn. Sheer insanity was stamped all over him. A deep and sticky darkness, like molasses syrup, oozed from Shaughn's pores. It settled on Micah's skin and body, like a cloud on a foggy day.

Micah wriggled in his chair. He was repulsed by the touch on his skin. Finally, completely losing it, he shouted at Shaughn, "I'm gonna send you back to the pit you came from! You're scum, Shaughn!"

Shaughn was unperturbed by Micah's show of temper. "Am I? You're in denial, Micah. You're living out your greatest fear. Aren't you?" Shaughn laughed. "Smoke and mirrors. Mirrors and smoke. Denial is very unbecoming of you. I thought you might be a worthy adversary. You're disappointing me, baby brother." Shaughn filed his perfectly manicured nails.

"Micah," a voice whispered in his ear.

Micah turned at the sound of the voice.

"Use your powers. Come with me, son," Weeping Willow said. She stood just outside of his line of vision. Her arms were outstretched. The tears fell in waterfalls.

"Come, son."

Slowly she drew Micah to her. There was blackness. A void. Then, Micah stepped into the recesses of another time and place. He was in the Victorian parlor. Only it wasn't the same. The furniture was arranged differently.

Directly in front of him was a mural on the center wall. A man and a woman were in the throes of ecstasy. Forbidden animal-like ecstasy.

Micah peered closer. A loud drumming sounded in his ears. Ocean waves frolicked, rolling through the inner recesses of his mind.

The man's foot was hanging off the sofa. Only it wasn't a foot. It was a hoof. It was a clawed hoof. Writhing underneath him was a beautiful woman, with flowing locks of dark thick hair. The woman in the mural was Evelyn's mother. She was Micah's grandmother.

Micah gasped.

Weeping Willow knelt before him. She stretched out her arms toward him. "Turn it around on him, Micah."

"Turn what around?"

"Just remember my words. Quentin Curry's greatest power is that of deceit."

Micah was confused. Before he could gather his thoughts she spoke again. "Help me."

Micah stared at the mural trying not to gag. "How?"

"Defeat him. The pureness of your heart will erase the sin. The only way you can beat him is if you believe."

"And if I don't?"

"Then we will all be damned. And he will win."

Micah broke down. "Why?"

"Jezebel. She's a powerful spirit. She possessed my body. She mated with him. I didn't know 'til it was too late. By that time he had implanted the creation for a perfect womb. Your mother."

Micah wept.

"There's one thing he didn't count on, Micah."

"What's that?"

"Repentance. I've been repenting since I made the discovery and a small miracle has occurred."

Micah got a hold of himself. "What miracle?"

"Quentin Curry is not your father." Weeping Willow began to fade. "You have been given great power. Go back, Micah, and right what's wrong."

"Grandma!" Micah yelled out but she was gone.

Chapter 43

Micah rebounded. His head ached. He was back in the basement. And he was still tied up.

The basement door creaked open. Quentin Curry entered. The dark, dankness of the basement faded in comparison to the presence of Quentin Curry. Diabolism seeped from the pores of his skin. Wickedness covered him in a sleek sheen. His very nature was animalistic. Looming disaster sizzled in the air.

His carriage was erect, full of supreme power. An air of arrogance encircled him. Scorching flames resided where his pupils would have been. Ruination, devastation and damnation sprung from his being, shuddering in the air.

The violation of the Ten Commandments was written in his essence. The instant he entered the room Micah knew hell was real. He was as close to hell as a person could ever come and still be alive.

Micah saw him for what he was. A third sight unfolded unto him. It allowed him to access what lay beneath Quentin's surface. The vision was so dynamic it rocked Micah in the chair he was bound to.

Millions of filmy clustered human images resided in Quentin. They screeched in eternal torment. They burned in damnation. Flames engulfed them, seared them, and scorched them.

They howled. Blistering boils covered their skin. They were seeking death. The second death eluded them. They suffered, in great agony. There was no relief.

Their parched, dry lips begged for water. They received not a drop. Then there was blood. There were buckets of it. It represented the stain of the blood of the Prophets. Quentin was wallowing in their blood.

He threw back his head and the blood bubbled up from his throat, blood from the past, his deceit of the Prophets.

The image altered. Zillions of maggots swarmed through his body. It was one form of fluid movement. A whirlpool blacker than midnight swallowed the maggots. Quentin's image transformed.

He was a beast with long strings of hair, scaly skin and beady little eyes. His feet were nothing more than clawed hoofs. Toothy fangs hung from his open mouth. Gobs of saliva ran like a stream, pouring from his lips.

He had wide flapping wings. Each was the size of a small mountain. Each was marked. Micah looked closer. The wings were embedded with an "X."

The beast hissed at Micah. Thick, yellow saliva dripped from its fangs. It bared its sharp, pointy teeth. Then a jelly substance formed on the body of the beast. The jelly made his body slick, oily and sleek.

The beast opened its mouth; unholy foam rose up and out of it. Then he spoke, "Worship me."

Micah saw the heads of people, more people than he had ever seen in his life bow before the beast. The beast opened his mouth devouring them whole. They joined the ones before them in eternal damnation.

Quentin smiled. Micah shut his eyes. He muttered under his breath, "My Jesus."

"It seems the entire brood of you insist on calling the name of a man who does not exist," Quentin said.

Micah narrowed his eyes. "He exists."

"Really?" Quentin looked amused. "Your grandmother didn't think so."

Micah spat at his feet. "You laid down with Jezebel, your own creation. You never touched my grandmother."

Quentin smiled. "Okay. I'll give you that. But, I had a heck of a time with your mother. Or shall I say my daughter."

Micah trembled. "If you force your presence on an unaccepting person and they repent, it sort of cancels you out. Doesn't it, Quentin?"

"Very knowledgeable, Micah. Perhaps, if they repented. I do stress the word if."

"My grandmother did."

Quentin's eyes turned to slits. "Your mother didn't."

"Funny," Micah said. "I seem to recall her calling out the name of Jesus! The day she called the reverend. You blanched in your spirit. Remember? You knew something was wrong but you couldn't stop it. The instant she beheld His name she scorched you. Like the demon you are. You erased His name from her memory. But, faith brought it back. When she remembered *His name* you were cancelled."

Quentin's tongue snaked out of his mouth like a lizard. An angry, hissing sound rose from his throat. Micah's sight was keener than he had given him credit for. How had he missed that? Someone was helping this boy.

"How did you know that?"

"I know a lot about you, Quentin. And now I have something to show you."

Micah flashed the images with the speed of light before Quentin's eyes.

Jezebel was in great travail.

Quentin's eyes became reptile slits.

"That which you sow in the spirit so shall you reap in the spirit, Quentin!"

Flowing from between Jezebel's legs was the head of a monster. Slowly it ejected from her womb, a baby beast, with fangs, claws and hoofs.

Quentin watched.

"You laid with Jezebel, Quentin. You mated with Jezebel. Here is the birth of the seed you implanted."

The hideous child slid completely out. It was fully formed. And there was no doubt it wasn't human.

"You can't very well reproduce and plant your seeds to become human from that. Now, can you, Quentin?"

Micah panted. He was in very deep.

Quentin's eyes were lit with livid malice. They were alive with pure venom.

Micah screamed at him. "Evelyn is her father's daughter, Quentin! Like I said what you sow in the spirit that shall you reap in the spirit! You lay with Jezebel. You produced with Jezebel! Not with my grandmother!"

Quentin squeezed Micah's throat. He didn't touch him. He simply reduced his oxygen supply. He let go. Micah gasped in air.

"There's still Shaughn," Quentin said.

"You won't reproduce through Shaughn either. He will die. He will die because he was born of a mortal woman. Sort of puts a kink in the plan. Doesn't it, Quentin?"

Malice ate its way through Quentin's body. It flew from Quentin's eyes. He had underestimated Micah's powers. The boy was not timid like his mother. He could kill him anytime he wanted. Instead he decided he would toy with him. It would give him great pleasure.

He stared at a chair located next to Micah. It burst into flames turning to ashes. Quentin watched Micah's expression as the chair burned. Micah thought about Silky bursting into flames.

"Yes, shame about Silky, isn't it?" Quentin said.

He absorbed Micah feeling him. He touched him. He touched him inside. He reduced the physicality of him. He had never liked what he saw. Micah reared back from his touch. The wires cut deeper into his wrists. Blood spurted.

Quentin said, "Whether you like it or not, Micah Jordan-Wells, you are my second son."

Quentin turned to look at Shaughn. "Shaughn is my first."

Shaughn merely smiled at Micah. He was extremely amused by the little father and son play that was going on. Touching little scene by what amounted to nothing more than demons. His turn would come.

"I ain't your son. I want you out of my house. I want you out of my mother's life." Micah paused, and then as if Shaughn were a mere afterthought, he added, "Oh, and take your bad seed with you."

"You're not a very gracious guest. Are you, Micah?" Micah's extreme arrogance was grating on Quentin's nerves.

Quentin moved a step closer to the chair in which Micah was bound. He was somewhat astonished at the nerve of a man who, while bound and helpless, still possessed the ability to display total arrogance.

Yet a part of him respected Micah's courage, although he was tired of his nonsense. He was tired of Micah Jordan-Wells. Period. It was time to extinguish him. It was time to destroy him. Yes, on this night he would be rid of him. Rid of him, and all that he thought he knew.

"I'm tiring of the game, Micah. So let me put it this way. You tried to step out of the world that's been created. Not your fault entirely. Your mother's for sure. But that cannot be, Mr. Detective. The twinning will take place. And you, Micah Jordan-Wells, will not stop it. You have no power here. Remember that. You can't be a hero in this story. There can only be one power. There *will* only be one power. It is prophecy. Micah, prophecy always comes to pass. Just as it is written."

Quentin moved another step closer to Micah. He was seething from the look in Micah's eyes. The boy was actually looking down his nose at him. With what?

What was that? Disdain. Quentin blanched.

"I wrote the book here, Micah. As such that makes me the author of what happens. So let me tell you what is going to happen to you. You're being written out. Extinguished. Gone. Disposed of. Do you get it?"

Micah evaluated Quentin. Something welled up inside him. A torrid velocity of words rang in his ears.

"You can't beat Quentin with the laws you work with."

"God is good. God is great."

"Turn it around, Micah." The "X" soared up before him.

"You can't beat Him if you don't believe."

Micah bowed his head. He whispered two words. "I believe."

With that he tapped into a raw supply of ethereal power. Quentin and Micah clashed for the power.

It was an almighty war. A war fought in the spirit. Only one of them could emerge with the victory.

Micah drew faith, a mighty, mighty faith. The old cross, made out of tree bark, stained with blood, rose from the depths of the earth. A thunderbolt screamed through the air. A flash of lightning streaked across the sky.

Day turned into night. Innocent blood spilled in the land. Micah finally knew. He knew what he had been given. And he knew why. He knew what he must do. The power to fight for innocence escalated in him.

Micah looked to his right. He saw a flash of brilliant, glittering white light. Quentin followed his gaze. He saw nothing. Quentin turned to look at Micah. He didn't like what he was feeling. There had been a shift in the balance of things. He could feel it.

Brightness in the form of a man stood before Micah. There were no features to his face. There was an astonishing, lustrous, shimmering light where His face would have been. He was dressed in a simple white robe.

His countenance was radiant, like the brilliant incandescence of the sun. It shined from the top of His head to the bottom of His burning feet. A striking golden glow settled in the basement. The light twinkled in Micah's direction.

There was only one power it could be. Micah had read and studied the scriptures at the reverend's knee when he was a young child. The power of the living words washed over him.

Never could he have imagined being in His presence. But, here he was. Micah knew it. A quiver shook his whole body. Tears sprung up, unashamed, and shimmered in Micah's eyes.

The light twinkled again. A pair of hands ascended from the light. Micah felt wetness on his face. The hands rose in ascension. Something splashed on him. The hands sprinkled him with holy water.

Dear Jesus!

Micah closed his eyes at the wonder of it. In that time, heaven and earth moved. There was a great rumble as though a bulldozer had pushed the house itself. Thunder cracked through the room.

Micah bowed his head. His hands were bound. He mentally crossed himself. He crossed himself with the sign of a man who had paid the price. He had paid the price in ridicule and blood.

Micah crawled down deep inside himself. He buckled the flesh. He tapped into spirit. Then he summoned a raw power that at one time he didn't know he had. It was time.

When he lifted his head he flipped the script. Micah looked up. His eyes sizzled. They scorched Quentin, scaling off a piece of his skin. Micah grabbed Quentin, shaking him like a rag doll. He tossed him clear across the room. Quentin crashed into the wall. He picked him up from the floor and tossed him like a leaf in the wind.

Quentin tapped his reservoir. He threw a fireball. It flew past Micah's head. He decided it was time for Micah to burn. He stared unadulterated hatred at him, intending to turn him to ash.

He mustered his supreme power, but Micah did not burn. He couldn't scorch him. He couldn't burn him. He couldn't turn him to ash. Quentin couldn't destroy Micah.

Quentin was raging. He waved his arms angrily in the air. It was impossible that this mere mortal could block his powers. But, block them he had. Quentin unleashed all of his mighty powers, the very depths of hell lashed out to scathe Micah.

Quentin stumbled into a dark discovery. He could not equal Micah. His powers had been stripped. He was trapped inside the body of a mere man. And Micah was holding the very thing that Quentin always used to tear men down with. He was holding the ultimate weapon. Micah Jordan-Wells was holding faith.

A deep ugly sound tumbled from Quentin's lips, "No! No! No!" He tossed Micah against the wall. A light streamed from Micah's eyes creating a wind tunnel. It swept Quentin up and banged him around like he was a toy soldier.

Quentin was on the losing end of the battle. Real fear gripped him as he realized a deception so deep, so ethereal, that his mind could hardly grasp it. The "X." It had been snatched. It was being held.

Micah hit Quentin with a gut-wrenching blow. "You're a thief, Quentin! You're a deceiver! Worse than that, you are a liar!"

"I am truth!"

"You are a fool!"

The agonizing "X" flamed between them. Quentin smiled in relief. It was back. Micah had made a mistake. The "X" was what made him eternal. It was his source of power.

Micah didn't blink an eye. He stared at the "X." It loomed up larger, brighter, burned more intensely.

Quentin stared at the power he had created. It was his mark. He willed it closer to Micah. It would scorch him just like in his dreams. Only this time it would burn him to ash. The tables were turned. He had the edge. Micah was too smart for his own good.

"Move," Quentin said.

The "X" didn't move. Quentin frowned.

Micah didn't flinch. He was no longer afraid. He had discovered the underlying foundation. Now he would rip it right out from under Quentin's feet.

Quentin issued an order. "Be doused." It didn't happen.

Glowing red coals seeped from the depths of his eyes, connecting with the "X." There was no scorching, no searing, no imprinting, no nothing.

"That is MY mark!" Quentin yelled at him. "I created it! Look at it! Everyone will know I was here!"

Micah smiled engagingly at Quentin. He showed him what was to come. Quentin trembled. Micah had found the source. Never before had anyone come close. Micah Jordan-Wells had tapped the well. In it was life. Real life.

Slowly, snail's pace slowly, Micah turned the "X." With each turn, a sharp stab of pain shot through Quentin's body. Piece by little piece he was being ripped apart.

Micah twisted the "X" a bit more, a flaming arrow pierced Quentin's side. He twisted it a little bit more. The next flaming arrow stabbed Quentin in the neck.

Quentin was burning, limb by limb. Miniature flames were eating up his body. He was nothing more than flesh warring against flesh. Micah gave the "X" a final turn. It righted. It righted into the shape of the cross.

It stood before Quentin, regal in all its humbleness. The cross was holy with all its power, majestic in all its pain, righteous and powerful in its origins. The cross simply impeded evil. It obstructed evil.

Quentin crouched. And he burned.

The "X" had inverted. Quentin's deception was played out. With this one revelation, Micah had stripped him to his core. Micah gave Quentin a last knowing look.

A light so bright streamed from his eyes that Quentin couldn't look at him. His face shimmered from the inside out.

Quentin covered his face. He winced from the light. Finally, he peeked out from his cover. What he saw made him bow his head.

Someone emerged from behind Micah. He was that light. Powerful was the presence of He. His countenance was radiant, like the brilliant incandescence of the sun. It shined from the top of His head to the bottom of His burning feet.

Quentin knelt down. He bowed paying homage to a power that was greater than his. He couldn't believe it. Another one. Another one connected to The King. Only this one was destined for great battles. He was marked. Grace was upon him. He would see him, again. It was written.

"Ashes to ashes and dust to dust, Quentin," Micah said. Quentin's body burst into flames. He disintegrated into the night.

Chapter 44

Quentin was gone. It was time to do battle with the last of Quentin's bad seed.

Micah struggled against the wires. Shaughn, who had been watching the battle between Quentin and Micah with heightened interest, laughed. He had a reason to laugh. With Quentin gone, the power was his. He had been assured of it.

Micah's little display of power was a two-edged sword. The Prophecy would be fulfilled, just as it had been declared.

"I guess that leaves you and me, little brother."

"I don't think so," Micah told him.

Micah's eyes turned into two black glowing coals shooting flames of fire. He focused on the wires binding his wrists. The wires snapped like broken toothpicks.

"Let the games begin," Shaughn said.

When the wires snapped, Shaughn shored up the walls around Micah turning them into mirrors. All around Micah was glass. All he could see was his own reflection. He couldn't tell where he began or where Shaughn ended.

Shaughn yelled out his name, "Micah!"

Micah raced toward the mirror image and the sound of Shaughn's voice. He touched nothing but glass. He heard Shaughn laughing.

Micah hit the glass in a fit of frustration shattering it. The sound of Shaughn's laughter continued to taunt him, seeping from the glass.

He ran from image to image, trying to connect with Shaughn. He hit the glass again, shattering his own image. Still he didn't come into contact with Shaughn. Then he heard Shaughn's voice behind him.

Micah turned. He came flesh to flesh with Shaughn. Micah and Shaughn grappled, inflicting bodily harm in brute force on each other.

Shaughn threw Micah to the floor. He straddled him and punched him in his face. He rained down blows like a madman, one after the other in fast succession, trying to destroy Micah's features.

Micah punched him back hard in the face. He returned blow for blow. His fist connecting hard and fast with a flesh that he hated. He tried to toss Shaughn off of him, but Shaughn was rooted in his position. Micah couldn't toss him.

Micah feigned trying to shield himself from the blows, not fighting back while inching his way to the fireplace with Shaughn on top of him. Shaughn was so engrossed with inflicting punishment on Micah he never noticed their bodies moving closer to the fireplace.

Micah's fingers strained and reached for the fireplace poker. Repeated, malicious blows continued to hammer away at his face. He reached the poker. He grabbed it. With a mighty thrust, he jammed the poker in Shaughn's Adam's apple knocking the wind out of him. Shaughn gagged.

In that edge of a second, he shoved Shaughn backward so hard that when he hit the cement floor air hissed from his body. Micah jumped to his feet. Enraged, he landed repeated blows with the poker to Shaughn's face and head. He rained down metallic blows with a force he hadn't known he was capable of.

Shaughn struggled to get up, then went for the low, grabbing for Micah's legs. He managed to grab one of them, but with his other leg Micah kicked Shaughn, knocking the wind out of him once again. Shaughn fell. He struggled to his feet and then, in a whirl as fast as a blur, he dropkicked Micah in the forehead. Micah fell and dropped the fireplace poker.

He scrambled across the concrete floor to retrieve it. Shaughn grabbed him. He held his legs trying to prevent Micah from reaching the poker.

They both reached for the weapon at the same time. With a burst of extraordinary strength, Shaughn tossed Micah to the side. He gained control of the poker. He swung it with fierce force. Micah dodged it.

Micah twirled around. He was lithe and full of grace, like a dancer in control of an extreme athletic grace. He threw his arms wide open in the air. The sound of thunder crashed through the room. The temperature dropped. Pieces of ice that looked like crystal formed in the air like frozen dewdrops.

Micah glared at Shaughn. He twirled again. He raised the temperature in the room to an unbearable degree. The heat was so intense it melted the furniture that had been stored in the basement.

Shaughn sweated profusely. Micah stared at the poker in Shaughn's hand. He willed it toward him. Shaughn tried to maintain his grip. He couldn't. He was nowhere near Micah's level of power. The poker floated out of his hand into Micah's.

Shaughn put his head down. He blindly rushed Micah. He fumed like a bull let loose in a corral. Micah dropped low. He hit Shaughn hard in the stomach. Shaughn screeched in pain.

Micah pulled Shaughn's head low. He kneed him in his nose. Bones cracked. He hit him with a deathblow in the neck. Bubbling vomit chortled in Shaughn's throat. Micah clapped his hands, hard over Shaughn's ears, causing phenomenal pain. Bursts of light exploded in Shaughn's head.

Shaughn was bruised. He was in extreme distress. He taunted Micah. "Raven is a good lay. She's a tasty little morsel. I enjoyed every inch of her and then some."

Micah kicked Shaughn in the mouth. He heard the sound of his teeth cracking. He kicked him in the mouth, again and again and again, oblivious to anything except his foot connecting with Shaughn's mouth.

Blood spewed forth from Shaughn's mouth like water from a fountain. He swallowed some of his teeth.

Shaughn stumbled. He licked his lips. His face contorted grotesquely as blood streamed from his mouth. He glared his hatred at Micah. He reached for Micah. But now he was hurting, as well as powerless.

As Quentin had done before him he tried to resurrect the "X." He summoned the source of his power. Criss Cross.

"The power is mine! It's mine!" he raged at Micah.

"Who's in denial now, Shaughn? The power is gone. It is no more."

Shaughn ignored him. He summoned the "X." The "X" didn't even rise. Shaughn had been disconnected from his power due to Quentin's defeat.

Micah knew it was time for the end. He would take Shaughn out of his misery. He swiftly turned the poker in the opposite direction. He stabbed Shaughn with all his might straight through the heart.

Shaughn's eyes opened wide in surprise and disbelief. More blood trickled from his mouth. He looked down as blood spilled out from the poker in his heart. He dropped to his knees. He keeled over. His body twitched in a strange death rattle, the mortality of a man's body dying swept over him.

Then he was gone.

Micah stared at the ashes of Quentin on the floor. He swept them into the burning fireplace. Flames shot up. They engulfed the ashes.

The thunder in the room ceased to roll. Micah looked up to see the brilliant light receding. It gave a final twinkle in his direction.

Evelyn was just awakening in the solarium when she saw the spirit of Shaughn reaching out his hands to her in a loving gesture. His alter was in place.

Vaughn said, "Why? Why did you give me away? Didn't you love me?"

A lone teardrop escaped from Evelyn's eye. It washed over the fatal "X" on the back of Shaughn's right hand. As the spirit of him floated away, she heard screeching like the sounds of many banshees.

He cried, "Mommy! Mommy!" one final time before he was sucked away.

In the basement Micah lifted Shaughn's right hand. He studied the "X" embedded in it.

Wearily he rubbed the back of his own head. His fingers never realized the barely perceptible number six embedded at the base of his neck. It was just below the hairline.

Both men were marked. Both men had inhabited the same womb. Both men had grown to be opponents in an ultimate war of the spirit, side by side.

The seed of the chosen one had already been implanted. The

seed had grown. One had been born of darkness; the other had been born to light. Micah hadn't received the chosen mark through a ritual. He had simply been born with it. The power of good had superceded evil from as far back as the womb.

Quentin's desire had been to eliminate any obstacles to his controlling earth when the time came. He wanted to thumb his nose at God and eventually take his throne.

His killing had been for naught. He sought to destroy the seed of the ones marked, so they couldn't produce a warrior. He had missed one very important element—he had not known the *time* of birth of the chosen one, nor the time of his conception. Nor had he expected it to be so close to home.

As he sought to destroy his coming, seeking to win by elimination the one whom had been chosen was already there in the form of Micah Jordan-Wells.

Quentin had lost the war the instant he started it. It had been lost to him in Evelyn's womb. Defeat had already been upon him.

He had also been wrong all along about the number six.

It had been turned against him. Just as his own power in the form of the "X" had been turned against him and converted into the sign of the cross.

All things belong to the Lord God! This has been in evidence since the miracle of creation at the beginning of time in the day of the Old Testament when He blew the breath of life from His nostrils. The number six was no different.

The mark of the beast is 666. Quentin felt power in that number. It was ultimately his mark. But, his own deceit had been turned against him and one six of the three, a single number had been chosen to represent good, and so it had.

It turned out to be an identifier of how good could overcome evil. Micah rubbed the base of his neck once again and then he sighed.

Long ago Evelyn had babbled out, "Jesus Lord! Jesus Lord! Jesus Lord!" in her fear of Quentin. That plea hadn't fallen on deaf ears.

The reverend had told her, "God has a way of working things out, child, in His time and in His way."

And so he had!

Chapter 45

Micah found Evelyn in the solarium. She was crying, softly. She rocked back and forth. Her arms were wrapped tightly around her shoulders.

He touched her tenderly on the cheek. "I know everything. It's over, Ma. Shaughn is dead. So is his father."

Micah hesitated. "There's no trace of Quentin's death. Thanks for telling Reverend Jackson to tell me. But you should have told me much earlier. I could have protected you. Why didn't you tell me the truth?"

Evelyn swallowed through her tears. She looked at Micah. "I was afraid. There are no records of him. No one would have believed me. There was nowhere to turn. I only ever stood up to him once, when I gave Shaughn away. I think Shaughn's not being here suited his plans anyway. If I had left or taken you away, he would have killed you. I couldn't bear that. Me, yes. But not you . . ." Evelyn's voice trailed off.

"You are the only good thing that came out of it," she said. "I couldn't bear to lose the one good thing in my life."

"I know about Grandma."

Evelyn flinched. It seemed Quentin had had his hands on her life for a long time. The depiction in the mural had been cruel. She had blacked out. When she had awakened she had told herself it was a bad dream. Micah's words told her it wasn't so.

"Quentin Curry isn't your father. He lay down with the spirit of Jezebel. He never touched Grandma. Grandma believed, Ma. Quentin couldn't destroy her faith. Her face and body were merely a mirage that Jezebel used. Quentin was a pawn in his own deception."

"How do you know that, Micah?" Evelyn searched the reins of his heart, as well as his eyes.

Micah thought of the brilliant light and all he had seen. "I know, Ma. Just trust me. I know."

Evelyn saw the truth of his words reflected in his eyes. She said nothing more.

Weeping Willow appeared behind Evelyn. She leaned over Evelyn's shoulder. She was finally free to go to her rest. She kissed her grandson on the forehead.

"You're a good boy, Micah. Keep the faith." She smiled. No more tears. Then she was gone.

Evelyn took Micah's face in her hands. She held him away from her. She traced the bruises on his face. She kissed his blackened, blue swollen eye.

"Micah, since Quentin's death can't be traced anyway, maybe we can keep it between us. People won't understand."

Micah locked eyes with Evelyn. He considered her words. He came to a decision. Finally, he nodded.

Evelyn wept. Dry sobs racked her body. She hugged Micah tightly to her chest. Micah cradled Evelyn in his arms. He rocked her like a baby, trying to comfort her.

Chapter 46

In her parlor, Evelyn poured herself a hefty shot of Chivas Regal. Micah, Wolfgang, and Nugent talked quietly among themselves. The police carried Shaughn's body out.

"This has been one hell of a case," Wolfgang said.

"Yeah. You can say that again," Micah replied.

Evelyn walked over to them. She offered a glass of scotch. Nugent took it. He gulped the liquid down in one swallow. Then handed the glass back to Evelyn.

He glanced at Micah and smiled. Micah smiled back. No words were needed. Their bond was solidified. A silent understanding floated between them.

Micah knew Nugent had demonstrated a loyalty to him that he couldn't have paid for. For that he was truly grateful. Nugent was just relieved to finally have the truth out. He was glad it was behind them.

Wolfgang looked at Evelyn. "Ms. Jordan-Wells," he addressed her with all due respect, "I'm afraid there is no way I can keep your name out of the press. This was one of the most twisted serial killer cases to ever go on the books.

"Micah is going to have to tell the truth. When he does, the press will be all over him. As I'm sure you know, there will be extreme focus on you as well. I am sorry, but I feel you need to be prepared for this."

Evelyn clasped both of Wolfgang's huge hands between her own. She gave him a direct look. "No. I am the one who should be sorry."

"Ma'am, you couldn't have had the power to stop this."

"One wonders sometimes, Wolfgang. I'm discovering that you can't run and you can't hide. I lost my faith. When you lose that you lose it all."

A look passed between Evelyn and Micah.

"And the truth is often stranger than fiction. Most people don't handle the truth very well," she said.

When Micah Jordan-Wells stepped out on the porch, flashbulbs exploded in his bruised and swollen face. He was just ahead of Wolfgang and Nugent.

Micah wore his bruises like a true soldier. The very pain of them was a reminder to him that there was something more in life.

The street was crowded with the police. The press was out in full force. Yellow rain slickers identified their ranks.

The Victorian house was being photographed from all available angles. Micah stood regal and proud on the porch. He watched the rain as it fell from the sky. He knew his life would never be the same.

He was the only one that heard the sigh of the Victorian, taking its final breath.

The Victorian house stood quietly. It would retain its own history. It would shield its secrets. Some of which would never be released.

Chapter 47

The reverend and Evelyn sipped coffee in Evelyn's parlor. The setting was befitting of a conversation they had long ago. Only a few things had changed.

Evelyn could hear the music again. She could feel the symphonic notes as they rose like waves crashing against the shore. Her spirit felt renewed. She was reborn. She had repented for her faithlessness. In doing so, she had reacquainted herself with her religion.

The cornerstone she had been reaching for so long ago had been Jesus Christ. But when she hadn't believed He was there, when she hadn't believed she could find Him, she hadn't. Then like a wisp in the night, He was gone. Erased from her memory for more than thirty years.

By His grace a great burden had been lifted from her shoulders. For the first time in years, her spirit was at peace.

The reverend smiled at the transformation Evelyn had undergone. Layers and layers of years, age, and most of all fear had been peeled away. She had emerged as a beautiful, bright star. She sparkled like a diamond.

He realized she was lit up from the inside. A golden glow emerged from her soul. She had been freed.

Evelyn allowed the reverend to immerse in his thoughts. She didn't venture forth with words. She was content to sip her coffee. It was not laced with Chivas Regal. She had discovered she didn't need the Chivas anymore. They sat in companionable silence.

When she felt the time was right, she said, "I don't know how to thank you, Reverend Erwin Jackson."

The reverend smiled at her use of his full name.

"Micah told me all about his visit with you."

The reverend shook his head. He did not acknowledge any credit due. "It is not me who needs to be thanked, Evelyn. I believe I mentioned long ago, God has a way of working things out, in His time and in His way."

Evelyn smiled. "Yes. I believe I have heard that from you before. Just the same, I am grateful for your faith. And most grateful for your friendship throughout the years."

The reverend nodded.

Evelyn's eyes grew serious. "Reverend, did you think Micah would survive?"

The reverend smiled. He thought back to the heat that had generated from the tree bark cross when he had been led to give it to Micah. "No, my dear, I didn't."

Evelyn shuddered.

"I didn't think Micah would survive. I knew he would. Your son, Micah Jordan-Wells, is chosen."

The reverend had seen the power in Micah's eyes. Justice between good and evil would be his plight. He thought about his plans in the ministry for Micah. Micah had his own agenda. So did Jesus Christ.

Evelyn stood up. She walked over to the drapes. She pulled them back a bit so she could look out the window.

"You know, Reverend, I believe it is time for a change." She pulled on the drawstrings of the heavy drapes. The room was immediately flooded with warm sunlight.

It was the first time the reverend had ever seen sunlight in the parlor.

Chapter 48

The following morning Evelyn stood in the foyer. She took deep breaths. She tried to conquer the last vestiges of her fear. It was fear that had gripped her and held her tightly in its grasp for more than thirty years.

She opened the door. She stepped out on the porch. She took a deep breath. That felt good. She couldn't believe it. She was actually outside the door. She smelled the autumn air. Hallelujah!

She squeezed her eyes shut tightly. When she opened them, she saw Micah across the street watching her. Warmth and encouragement flowed from his eyes.

Micah's heart turned over in his chest at the sight of his mother on the porch. It was her first taste of freedom and fresh air. It was an act of courage. He had been graced to see it. He nodded past the lump in his throat, grateful for the sight.

Micah had battled his mother's demons. In doing so, he had set her free. His eyes stung behind his lids. He blinked.

Evelyn smiled at her accomplishment. She was like a baby who had discovered she could take her first step without help, realizing the freedom mobility would bring.

Evelyn let out a deep breath. She closed the door softly behind her. She took a tentative step. Tears welled in her eyes. Micah held his breath. Shakily, she took another. Her heart hammered against her chest. Her limbs trembled with the effort.

Silently, Micah cheered her on. *Come on, Ma, you can do it.* Evelyn reached the banister and held on tightly, she paused for a moment. She closed her eyes. She was actually feeling fresh air, a breeze on her skin. The darkness in her life was being lifted like a veil. My Lord! She placed her foot on the first step down.

Micah felt wetness gliding down his cheeks as he watched her. One step. Two steps. She was on the pathway. Taking a deep and final exhilarating breath, she put one foot in front of the other, and on shaky legs she began walking across the street to join her son on the sidewalk.

Micah exhaled. When she reached him, Evelyn wiped the wet residue of tears from her son's cheek. Her own tears flowed freely. Both she and Micah reached for one another at the same time, hugging each other tightly. For a moment, Evelyn just held him, listening to the rapid beat of his heart that was thumping against her ear. She saturated his shirt with her own tears.

Micah smoothed the locks of her hair in a gentle rhythmic motion. Then he gave her a tight squeeze. When finally they pulled apart, Evelyn looked deep into Micah's eyes and said, "You're a brave boy, Micah. Thank you."

"Not necessary," he said, "you're an extraordinary woman. You always have been." Then he took her hand in his.

Together they stood looking at the house. Rumblings of the past swarmed Evelyn, swamping her in emotion. She had suffered, but in the end she had triumphed. She had won. Blessed be the name of the Lord!

Coming to a final decision she said, "I'm donating the house to the Historical Society. It's one of the last of its type in Newark. I hope you don't mind," she told Micah.

Micah hugged her. "No, Ma. I don't. But listen up. Today I want to do something special with you."

"Oh, yeah. What's that?" Evelyn asked.

Micah looked at her tenderly. A bright smile broke out on his face. "Take a walk. I want to take a walk with you."

Evelyn smiled too. She blinked back the tears that threatened once again to spill from her eyes. It would be the first walk she had ever taken outside with her own child.

Micah grabbed her hand. Together they walked along the leaf-strewn street. They left the old Victorian house behind.

Evelyn and Micah laughed like two children out for a day of freedom. They enjoyed the sheer comfort of each other's company. Evelyn reveled in the sheer feel of the breeze blowing her hair. Today her hair flowed free. She had dispensed with the long, thick, locked braid she liked to wear. She giggled like a kid.

They passed the park. Evelyn saw a familiar figure sitting on one of the benches feeding the pigeons. It couldn't be. But in her heart she knew she would never forget him.

She watched his movements. There was something about the grace of his hands and the tilt of his head. His litheness shone through, even in ragged clothing. No. Yes.

The man lifted his head. He made eye contact with her. Evelyn stared directly into his eyes. In a flash, she saw a reflection of Micah.

Suddenly, like a fish shedding its scales, something locked into place for her. Her thoughts raced across more than thirty years. Oh my God! How could it be?

She knew it was true. His testament stared her in the face. She caught her breath quietly. She didn't break her stride. She didn't want to alert Micah.

Her cherished son was not born of the seed of Quentin Curry. Something had taken place. Something had altered the events of things. In the alteration she had been handed a precious gift.

The man winked. She saw the imprint of who Micah was stamped all over him. He nodded in Micah's direction. He lifted two fingers in peace. Then he tilted the brim of his raggedy derby hat over his eyes. He continued to feed the pigeons.

Evelyn looked away. When she looked back he was gone. She scanned every inch of the park. There was no sign of him. There was also no sign of the pigeons he had been feeding.

The reverend's words rang in her ears. "Your son, Micah Jordan-Wells is chosen."

Evelyn felt blessed and burdened. Burdened and blessed. Silently she dedicated her life and her son's life to the Lord.

Evelyn looped her arm a little bit tighter through Micah's. He looked down at her and smiled. The shadow of secrets had finally been laid to rest for her.

Chapter 49

Raven stood nervously outside Micah's door. She bit her bottom lip. She paused. Finally, she pushed the door open.

Micah watched her as she walked through the door. She hesitated. Her steps faltered. She willed her legs to move, first one and then the other.

Tentatively, she risked a look from under her lashes at Micah. She found he was smiling that beautiful, sexy, melt-your-heart-away smile that she loved so much. She looked into his eyes, seeing the warmth and compassion they held. He opened his arms wide to her. Raven flew into them.

Scalding hot tears drenched Micah's cheek. Micah held her tightly. The love, the agony, as well as the desolation he had experienced because of Raven washed over him. It was reflected in his face. He took a step back. He put her at arm's length so he could look at her.

He reached into his pocket. He pulled out a small, exquisite box. "If you promise to stop drenching me, then maybe I can give you the rock."

A smile lit up Raven's face.

Micah opened the little black box. Sitting on black velvet, in all its power, was a perfectly cut, pear-shaped diamond, holding its own at 3.5 carats.

It reflected fractions of light. The light was nowhere near as bright as Raven's eyes.

Micah wiped away Raven's tears. He slipped the ring on her finger.

"Did you find a castle for me to be king of?"

"Yeah," Raven swallowed over the lump in her throat, "I know just the place."

"Good," Micah told her.

Then he got down on bended knee. He asked the question that Raven had been longing to hear: "Will you marry me, Raven?"

Raven searched his eyes. Finding what she was looking for she told him, "Yes. Yes, Micah, I will."

Micah rose and took her in his arms.

He had seen the dark side of evil. He had seen the light. He had seen the most major theft in the universe committed. Then he had witnessed restoration. He had decided life was worth living.

He knew a man's darkest moment was sometimes his greatest moment of strength. The only way to win was by fighting on the right side.

Chapter 50

The reverend reclined in his library. He mulled over the recent events. He looked at another photo of Micah Jordan-Wells on the front page of the newspaper. The picture had been taken the night Micah had vanquished Quentin. The night he had silenced Shaughn. Peace had been restored.

The reverend studied the photograph. He saw the clear light that leaped from Micah's eyes in spite of his bruised face. He didn't think Quentin and Shaughn would be the last dragons Micah slayed. Micah was on the path to justice.

He got up. He wandered around the library, touching the binding of different Bibles, books, and sermons that lined the shelves. He wondered if in them was some kind of answer that lay beyond them all.

He went back to his desk. He looked at the picture of Micah once more. He folded the newspaper in half. He knew this wouldn't be Micah's last battle. Some people were born to fight. Their births were sometimes like an invisible catalyst to change.

The reverend filed the newspaper away in his drawer under Evelyn's name. This was the last chapter in an overpowering saga. He locked the drawer.

He selected one of the ancient-looking Bibles that stocked the shelves. He settled in his easy chair for some scriptural studying.

He flipped open the flap and said, "Hmmm, yes, through the history of time, there have been many warriors. According to Your will, Father; according to Your will."

The reverend sighed. He settled back in his easy chair for a dose of the day's wisdom. He decided to read the book of Proverbs.

Chapter 51

Evelyn looked up at the cathedral in Newark. It was a majestic, awe-inspiring structure. It reached high toward the sky. It was located in a part of Newark where it was truly most needed.

The area skirted the edge of Branch-Brook Park, renowned for its cherry blossoms. It boasted an old state building, a roller skating rink, and housing projects that had been closed down due to the vast amount of bodies that had been found in its hallways, on its steps, and in its garbage Dumpsters over the years.

There were blocks of ordinary residences and corner stores. The streets were littered with kids, yelling and screaming in a kaleidoscope of culture and different languages.

The boarded-up windows of the projects and the dilapidated area were in stark contrast to this structure, which was regal and proud in its standing.

Evelyn idly wondered if any of the squatters, who surely must inhabit the closed-down projects, had ever looked out through eyes that had seen it all and wondered if there were something or someone residing in the cathedral that could really help them.

She wondered if they ever reached out from behind the grunge and the wasteland of their lives. Did they even know about faith and its power? She hadn't.

A familiar feeling washed over her at the thought. She recognized it as despair. It was a feeling she had lived with for a long time. She sighed. Now it was all behind her. She knew she must take one step at a time. She had to put one foot slowly in front of the other, into the future.

The haunting sound of Vaughn's voice never left her. She could hear it in her head. She heard it when she was awake. She heard it when she was asleep. The child she had borne had been caught in a web of deceit. A part of him had longed to be free. She shook her head at the devastating futility of it all.

Evelyn climbed the stairs to the cathedral. Slowly she walked down the red-carpeted aisle. She gazed at the sun's rays reflecting through the stained glass windows.

She went to the altar and lit four candles. One was for Micah. One was for her. One was for Reverend Erwin Jackson. The last and final one was for her child who never grew, Shaughn Braswell. She prayed in silence.

Her next stop was the cemetery where she laid one single white lily on the grave of Shaughn Braswell. She knew she was the only one who would ever shed a tear over his passing. That single fact in itself made her sad.

Through his death she had grown into a forgiveness that she never would have thought herself capable of. She had lived in bondage for more than thirty years. She still didn't understand it all.

But, her wounds were healing. She must heal. It was the only way to go on. It was the only way she could continue to hear the music, the symphonic notes, which drew the linear outline to her being.

Evelyn walked slowly out of the cemetery. She did not look back. It was the last time she would ever visit. However, it was not the last time the haunting voice of a little boy would call out to her: "Mommy! Mommy!" Not even the power of the grave could silence that voice.

For a moment in time, she saw Shaughn flash a grin. She heard Vaughn asking for raspberry sherbet. With a mother's heart, she wondered what it would have been like had things been different.

What if she had had the strength to fight the evil? Instead of being paralyzed with fear, instead of giving in to it? Would things have been different? It was a question she would never know the answer to.

Like a pawn on a chess table, she had only been able to make the moves that were given to her. They were limited in their capacity. There were other pieces that had more power.

Evelyn closed the gate to the cemetery. She walked the dirt path that led out to the street. When she reached the street, a van went by. Written on it was a slogan that read: "New Beginnings."

Evelyn smiled. She walked down the street. "New beginnings," she whispered in the wind.

Chapter 52

Micah and Nugent were across the street from the Prudential Center watching a towering spray of water shoot up from the fountain. The laughter and silly games of the kids getting out of school resounded in the air around them. It was a good sound.

Nugent picked up a rock. He threw it into the fountain. "You know, I was really worried about whether you would make it out alive."

"I know. So was I. Until I found out that the things you don't see are the most profound."

Nugent glanced at Micah from the corner of his eye. He sensed a change in him. He still looked like Micah, but there was a different layer to him. He couldn't quite put his finger on it. But it was there.

There was something in the way he moved. The way he looked. He looked the same. There was just a different quality to his looks.

"Well, I hope we see whatever monsters are destined to come our way in the future. Somehow I just feel more comfortable when I can see them."

Micah frowned. He turned to watch some kids bouncing a basketball. "That's the thing, Nugent. The most powerful enemy is the one we don't see. The one we don't believe is there."

Nugent scrutinized him. "You getting deep on me, man?"

"Naw. It's just an observation, Nuggie. Just an observation."

Chapter 53

Micah sat in the dark room with its vast ceiling. His mind raced. The images kept banging away, dancing in front of his eyes.

He'd been inside the dark tunnels of the minds of too many killers. Where did they end? Where did he begin? It was a futile question.

His skill lay in the ability to delve into their minds. He was a man walking in a dark cave, but he knew every crevice, every cragged step and nuance.

Inside their skin, he became one with them. The air they breathed seared his lungs. Their thoughts tumbled through the vast valleys of his conscience. He peered at the victims through their eyes.

It was an eerie place to be. He was tired.

Maybe he should tell Wolfgang he couldn't be the star boy anymore. He was not the Dragon Slayer. He could no longer trade pieces of his soul with killers.

The level of darkness he had stepped in had gotten to him. Then there was Raven. She had experienced ruthlessness at its deepest depths. And he couldn't prevent it. She had become a target because of him. Used to place a stamp that would forever sear his soul, although she would never know the truth of that.

He was going to marry Raven and he wasn't sure if he could continue to subject her to the terrors of his work. He wasn't sure he could risk losing her, because at risk she would definitely be. She was a part of him. To have her wrenched away by an evil that was uncontrollable would be unbearable. It would rip him apart. How? How could he continue to risk her?

Serial killers were natural hunters. In this last case, he had been the hunted not the hunter. It had taken a supreme power to save him.

Every time he came up against one of them, he was always left with the feeling that someone had opened up his body, shook everything out, and left nothing but the shell. The killers left the imprint of their signatures indelibly stamped on his spirit.

He sighed. In the silence of the night, he was the only one that heard them, the cries of the victims, the raging of maniacs, the brutality slashed across a canvas in all its bloody gore. They plagued his dreams.

The truth was painful. It did not always set you free. It carried a burden, a dedication, and an obligation. The truth had transported him from his everyday world. It had set him in a realm that most people never see.

He should get out of the streets. He needed to get out with his mind, body, and soul intact. He needed to get out while there was still a chance to get out. His life was like an urban thriller.

But some things in life couldn't be escaped. And some gifts couldn't be refused. As he sat there in the darkened room with its vast ceilings, once again it was upon him.

A man screamed, howled and jerked in the spasms of agonizing pain. Again, a visionary manifestation in the flesh transported him to the scene. Like a caged bird on an airline flight, he was there.

Micah's hand trembled with each slice of the knife, as it ripped and gouged the skin of the victim. Blood spurted as he carved out two trophies. He dropped them in a cellophane bag.

Tossed back into his own skin, frame by frame, shot by shot—in his mind's eye he saw the latest killers prancing in their supreme arrogance. Leaving a trail that could not be forgotten. Silky, Shaughn, and Quentin. They represented the elite power of Criss Cross. They were by far the most sadistic, powerful killers he had ever witnessed. And in them had been damnation.

The lights came on in the vast room, shattering the darkness. The curtains rolled slowly shut. The audience rose from their seats in a hushed silence. The kind of silence you get when people are stunned and don't quite know what to say.

Sirens shrilled in the distance. It was the symbol of vision and reality clashing. Micah stood up. He relived his recent descent into hell. Criss Cross was a quest for power at its most supreme. Criss Cross was an illusion, an image.

The greatest way to destroy a man was to create an image of a world he couldn't live in, because in his mind, that world became real.

When he had stepped into Quentin and Shaughn's illusions, he had had to tap into a belief that was rooted in the core of his being. He had tangoed with Satan. Face to face. Enough was enough.

The sirens were getting closer. Reality was racing toward him.

The ushers started down the aisles sweeping up popcorn and picking up soda cups. Micah watched the credits roll by for a story he had not seen. The only story he had seen was the one of his life.

The title, "Criss Cross" flashed in bright blood-red across the screen.

Micah shut his eyes. When he opened them the words were gone. The credits rolled normally. The soundtrack thumped.

He knew it would be a long time, if ever, before he got over Criss Cross. It was too personal and too close to home. It was a spiritual journey, a fight not of the flesh, but of the spirit. The prize at stake had been his soul. He had come face-to-face with damnation, and survived.

His cell phone rang. Micah clicked on.

"Micah, I need you on this. We have two dead rival gang members. They're tied to a tree. Together. They've been cut up pretty badly. Their throats have been slashed."

For an instant, Micah thought about getting out and saying "No."

But he had been given a gift. He had to use it. The fight for justice swelled up inside him. He had tapped into the greatest belief in the world, and found it to be true. He owed a debt.

"You're a good boy, Micah. Keep the faith." The words of his grandmother touched his spirit.

"I'm on my way," Micah said.

The path had been laid. He was a champion. He hadn't seen the most powerful light in the world so he could turn away. No matter what he thought, there really wasn't a choice. The choice had been made for him.

He'd received an extraordinary sight at the third level. Not merely a second sight, but a third. It was rarely heard of. He couldn't run from the darkness. He had to stand up to it. That was how he had won the battle. Criss Cross was only the first round.

Wolfgang's voice brought him back into focus. "Micah, there's one more thing."

"What's that?"

"The gang members. Both of their eyes have been cut out. There's a note that reads: 'Eyes that see, but have no sight.'"

Micah tucked the cellophane bag in his pocket. He couldn't yet see who he was.

CRISS CROSS

EVIE RHODES

ABOUT THIS GUIDE

The suggested questions are intended to enhance
your group's reading of CRISS CROSS by Evie Rhodes.

DISCUSSION QUESTIONS

1. Criss Cross is a power. Where is it derived from?

2. How did Evelyn develop agoraphobia?

3. How could Evelyn have handled her situation differently?

4. What criteria did Quentin use to select Evelyn to give birth?

5. Could Reverend Erwin Jackson have advised Evelyn differently in the beginning?

6. What was the one trait that was out of character for Silky?

7. How did Micah's birth come about?

8. What was Micah's salvation?

9. How was Micah affected by his dead grandmother?

10. What does the ending of Criss Cross mean?